Book I of the Austen Gaskell Series

Curiosities & Contemplation

A 'Pride & Prejudice' and 'North & South' Variation

NEY MITCH

Greetings, Readers!

As we all are aware, in Regency England, there was a famous writer named Jane Austen.

During Victorian England, there was another famous writer by the name of Elizabeth Gaskell.

Jane Austen went on to have one of the most legendary posthumous careers in the history of novelists. While gaining a faithful audience, her fame was launched to new heights throughout the 20th century and continues to this very day. Very rarely can a person go more than three streets without there being someone who knows of her writing and her genius.

Next came Elizabeth Gaskell. While she was noteworthy and well-received throughout her life, her writing would go on to diminish over the years, and she would gain less prominence compared to Miss Austen. Her writing would soon be given a resurgence of notice when BBC adapted three of her popular works: *Wives & Daughters*, *North & South*, and *Cranford*. These were the means through which I was introduced to Miss Gaskell's works. Over the years, quite a few of us have begun to compare the similarities of Miss Austen's second published novel to Miss Gaskell's *North & South*.

Since I owe a great deal to the *North & South* BBC adaptation, adapted by talented writer, Sandy Welch, I could not begin without giving credit for where credit is due. Of course, I couldn't help but get my mind working and wonder what it would be like if Miss Austen's characters met Mrs. Gaskell's. Ergo, this is a *Pride & Prejudice* Reimagining that also includes the characters from *North & South*. Rest assured, the reader does not have to have read *North & South* to understand this novel, though I would recommend watching the BBC miniseries, for it is quite a compelling adaptation!

To bring both worlds together, this story will take place during Victorian England. However, rather than adhere to 'Victorian' values, I will still add a touch of the Regency tone, when it comes to how women and men interact. Also, whenever a chapter focuses on Elizabeth, the narrative tone is in the first person, and when chapters focus on other characters, it switches to the third person voice.

Now, I hope you shall enjoy the Second Edition of this series. Originally, the First Edition was published in 2020, to not confuse readers who had partaken in the series four years ago. Also, there is an Afterword at the end of the book, to answer any questions that the reader might have.

Thank you for being willing to consider this reimagining and I hope that you enjoy yourselves. Once more, I dedicate this book to you, the reader, for being darn brilliant!

I also wish to give a special thanks to my parents, Helyn Roberts-Vickers, Miss Novo, and A. Madison for still supporting this wayward writer!

Now read on, dear friends, read on...

Ney Mitch

Chapter 1

The Departure

I t is a tendency, universally experienced, that one sometimes cannot fall asleep when one is awaiting a daunting event the next day.

No matter how comfortable the bed, how kind are the occupants who live at the residence where you rest, how lovely the room that you sleep in, you will remain there, staring up at the ceiling, with the darkness like a weight around you.

Such was I. Every part of my skin felt as if individual pins and needles were pricking it, daring me to fall asleep, while making it impossible to do so.

Every part of my soul was filled with questions and doubts about tomorrow. After all, it was the first day toward a future that was undecided, undefined, and untamed. Most of my life had been so well-regulated, so confined within a set of proper parameters, that I never believed there would be any change in my life.

Although all the signs were there, all the warnings were given, tragedy does not strike you as being something that will affect you—until it does.

And then, you had one option as a young lady of hardly any

fortune to her name, of very little to live on, and no dowry of any kind. You had to marry well or begin to do that thing that many people do not find desirable: you had to find your profession and hoped that all chances would fall into place.

Your future is bleak because it is just so unknown. Your solace is visiting friends.

Whatever differences I have with Edith Shaw—forgive me, now Edith *Lennox*, I adore her and knew that I would miss her company terribly. She had the open temper that suited me well as a companion and was a constantly loyal friend.

I would even miss the whirlwind that surrounded her wedding.

I would miss how safe I was in this house.

How I felt that there was nothing to worry over while I was here.

Even all the days where I had to be taken up by events and social visits that I had no control over—those same events that I would internally rail against because I was never consulted on what I wished to do—now seemed so charming and inviting.

After all, necessary obligations are always more endurable than the unknown.

But tomorrow brought the very unknown before my feet. And my mind could not rest, on both fear and expectation of where my life was going to be headed towards.

"Oh, Elizabeth, I wish that you would stay and accompany us," Edith said, as the servants began to convey my luggage out of my room and into the chaise and four.

"Selfishness is a common failing," I responded, smiling sadly, "and I have it. Yes, I do wish I could go with you. But in this case, I'm going to do everything in my power to ignore that wicked side of myself."

"You are not wicked," Edith said, "and wait there."

She left my guestroom and returned, carrying two Indian shawls. Reading her mind instantly, I prepared my refusal.

"Oh, Edith, I couldn't!" I cried, but she ignored my pleas.

"No, I will not be denied," she argued, unfolding the shawls, and then laying each one on both sides of my shoulder. "If you are to leave me and join Margaret in the North—oh, the dreaded North—then I will give you both a gift of color and something fine to remember me by." She leaned into me, conspiratorially. "I don't care what Uncle Hale says... I've heard the worst things about Milton. They say that the town has one color to it: gray. Gray, gray, gray!"

I laughed.

"I'd say that you are exaggerating," I noted, "but this time, I shall have to plead ignorance and admit that you may know something that I do not."

"How delightful! For the first time ever, I can claim to be the authority on this matter." She steered me toward the mirror, so that I could see the shawls better. "There, my gift to you and Margaret."

"You know your cousin better than I," I said, "you know which shawl would suit her better."

"You know her as well as me. Now, choose your favorite and Margaret will have the other as a gift."

"Oh, the decision must be left to me?" I remarked, looking in the mirror. "And now I must be selfish."

There was a knock on the door and we both turned to who was the intruder. Our faces relaxed as we saw that it was Edith's new husband, Captain Lennox. Lennox was a tall and handsome man, in his late twenties and with all the charm to go with his looks.

"What is this?" Captain Lennox asked, amused as he walked up to us. "Miss Elizabeth, this is your day of departure and you and my perfect bride are acting like you are preparing for a dinner party."

"From dinner party to departure," I said to him, "you must

allow ladies to be ladies. I refuse to believe that your taste in women was not so experienced that you didn't know what you were marrying."

"He did indeed know what he was marrying," Edith said, resting her chin on my shoulder.

"And I would have it no other way," Captain Lennox responded. "Miss Elizabeth, first Miss Margaret Hale leaves my wife and now you."

"Margaret and I left with no desire to abandon a good friend," I urged him to believe. "Margaret's duty was to family and mine is to life. Now, I believe that Edith wants you to decide a matter for both of us."

"Indeed, I do," Edith responded, going up to him and taking his arm. "This is your chance to see how proficient you are in ladies' fashions."

"Now what would a lowly captain like me know about that?" he asked, amused. As I put my last item in my carpet bag, I looked on them both as they stared into each other's eyes.

From Edith's lovely and charming face, framed by her perfect blonde curly hair, to Lennox's tall frame, they were perhaps the most handsome couple in London. Neither one of them were people of great information nor deep thought, but that was why I liked them. Altogether, they were the model of a happy couple who I was aware possessed a love that might never reach me. When looking on them, I knew that one thing was certain: they were the model of an ideal marriage.

How different it was to a year ago, when I beheld my elder sister, Jane, who was in the very throes of love with a man who would have made a marriage worth the earning. However, that match never came to be, and all my hopes were dashed against the rocky grounds of Fate. Now, I had Edith and Captain Lennox as the ideal model, and they were living up to the few matches in the world that I could admire.

With the rest of us, life was constantly playing a cruel joke—

a hope for an ideal love or life that would always be just out of our reach. But here, on Wimpole Street, London, a dream did come true. I had that knowledge as a warmth that often revived my faith in Man.

Once they stopped looking longingly into each other's eyes, Captain Lennox turned and analyzed the shawls that were draped across each of my shoulders.

"I am to decide which one looks best on you," he determined.

"And the other will go to Margaret," Edith clarified.

"Well, I have only one lady before me, so I shall oblige." Captain Lennox walked up to me, scrutinizing the craftwork that went into each shawl. At last, he pulled the one that was on my left shoulder.

"This is the one for you," he declared. "Margaret shall look splendid in the other one." He turned to Edith. "How did I do?"

"Splendidly! What do you think, Elizabeth?" Edith asked me.

"I think he passed the test," I surmised.

"I was being tested?" Captain Lennox asked.

"This is women's fashion; of course, you were being tested!"

We were interrupted by Mrs. Shaw, Edith's mother.

"Oh, Poor Elizabeth!" She declared. "Here come the bad tidings. Your luggage is packed away in the carriage and is ready for departure."

Walking up to her, I pressed her arm lovingly with my hand and kissed her cheek.

"I will miss how you always call me Poor Elizabeth whenever you had bad news to tell me."

"You will miss us, surely."

"Of course, I will."

They escorted me downstairs as I put on my coat, scarf, bonnet, and gloves.

When done, I took one last look at everything.

"I will never forget how you have helped me recover since mama's passing," I said to Mrs. Shaw and Edith.

"She was my dearest friend," Mrs. Shaw said, "when your mother left this earth, you lost much. I know the feeling of losing a mother, and I knew that it would be especially harder on you girls. No offense to your father, of course."

"I understand." I smiled wistfully. "You must not blame him for dying too early, Mrs. Shaw. He couldn't control that."

"I know. God bless him, but you know my sentiments on the matter. I will always believe that he should have done a better job at providing for your future. And now, Mr. Hale is doing the same thing with poor Maria and Margaret."

I let her say what she wished because it was wrong to try and contradict her.

"Say what you will," Mrs. Shaw continued, "but when I had to marry General Shaw, the disparity of age difference between us was too trying for me to ever be happy. I did what I had to do so that Edith would escape my fate."

"Mama, Elizabeth doesn't need to hear this again," Edith said, rolling her eyes.

"She does, however, for her father should have made certain that his daughters could have the same chances in life. I used to say that he did not help you five by letting you all loiter away on Longbourn without gaining more connections in town. A good thing it was that your mother made sure that you all learned a trade, so you all could provide for yourselves. Though, in my opinion, it should have never come to that."

"I will manage. But I thank you."

"And I do believe that she would have," came a voice behind us.

We all turned, and it was Mr. Henry Lennox, Captain Lennox's brother.

"Sitting still and doing nothing has never been Miss Bennet's style," he determined.

"Henry!" Captain Lennox called. "I worried that you wouldn't arrive in time."

"You have underestimated me, brother," Mr. Lennox said, coming up to us, "punctuality is a requirement of my profession. If it were not that, I would never win a case."

Mr. Henry Lennox and his brother, the Captain, were physical and mental contradictions. Captain Lennox got the larger share when it came to handsome looks. Mr. Henry Lennox was not very handsome at all, though his appearance was not altogether unpleasant. Yet his mind and tendencies were very shrewd, and he was a clever attorney, while his brother's mind didn't lend itself to any sort of business-like inclinations. Rather, Captain Lennox was made for a military life and his brother was made for a mental one. Overall, I still liked the Captain the most.

"Henry!" Mrs. Shaw said. "Timely met. Do you have all that you need for the journey?"

"Very much so, madam," Mr. Lennox responded, "my bags are placed in the chaise already." Finally, he turned to me. "So, Miss Elizabeth, I am to be your chaperone."

"I wish I could say that we will get along charmingly," I uttered, lightly, "but how is one ever to know?"

We walked out to the chaise, and he offered me his hand when I got in. Next, he climbed in himself, and we looked down at the family that we were leaving behind.

"Edith and Mrs. Shaw," I pressed, "do you still have my letter to Charlotte Lucas?"

"Yes, I do," Edith assured me. "I will mail it to her today."

"Thank you," I said, and my eyes grew wistful. "I will miss you all."

"And we shall miss you, dear," Mrs. Shaw said.

"Elizabeth!" Edith urged, and she had that conspiratorial look in her eye that I knew I would miss. Leaning forward, I pressed my ear closer to her lips so that she could whisper the secret that she was about to tell me.

"In case you ever see Mr. Darcy again...be kinder to him. I still think you should have accepted his offer."

I looked at her sincerely.

"You know that I couldn't," I said, "and I still feel that I was right."

"I know," she responded, "but I still can't help it."

"I know. This is just you caring for me."

"Precisely."

At last, we said our final farewells, we closed the carriage doors, and we were off.

"I was told that we are stopping briefly at Cheapside," Mr. Lennox clarified.

"Yes," I said. "I promise, we will be there for no more than a quarter of an hour to twenty minutes. I just need to say farewell to my sister, Mary. Due to her schedule, she couldn't come to the house to visit me before I left."

"And she works in your uncle's factory?"

"Yes. He's my Uncle Gardiner. He lives only a street away from his factory, and Mary was the most skilled at learning the work there. Her attentiveness paid off and she lives with them. But it all worked out for the better because they only had one bedroom to spare."

"Because they have children?"

"Four of them. Two girls and two boys. Susan, Ruth, Daniel, and Nathan. They are dear children. And it is no wonder. My Aunt and Uncle Gardiner are very elegant sort of individuals, like Edith and Mrs. Shaw. When meeting my uncle, you would not think him any less than a gentleman, despite him being a tradesman."

"Many tradesmen have been known to be better than how they are depicted as."

"And what of tradeswomen?" I asked, with a raised eyebrow.

His eyes twinkled, comprehending my meaning.

"Yes. We must not forget them, must we?"

"No," I confirmed. "We must not."

We rode along and very soon, we reached Cheapside.

When we arrived, I saw Mary's face in the window on the second floor. Since she already knew to expect me, she didn't wait till I entered, but came out of the door as Mr. Lennox offered me his hand to let me down from the chaise.

"Elizabeth!" Mary exclaimed. Her raised voice surprised me, because Mary was usually never prone to raising her voice louder than common volume.

"Oh!" I replied as she embraced me, and I folded my arms around her. "Now this is happiness to see me."

"Yes, it is," Mary said, then she turned to Mr. Lennox.

"Mary," I introduced, "this is Mr. Henry Lennox, Captain Lennox's brother."

"And now also having the good fortune to be Edith's brother-in-law," Mr. Lennox said, bowing.

"Mr. Lennox, this is my sister, Mary Bennet."

"Good day, Mr. Lennox," Mary said, curtsying. When she did so, she noticed that her dress was a little wrinkled. "Forgive me, for you have not caught me at my best. I've been working in my uncle's factory."

"I begrudge nothing," Mr. Lennox replied. "I too am tied down to my profession."

"Let us go inside and you both can learn more about each other," I said, taking Mary's hand.

We entered my uncle's home, but he was not there. Rather,

Aunt Gardiner was, and her children were all upstairs, preparing to come down to greet us.

"Mr. Lennox," I said, "this is my aunt, Miss Miriam Gardiner."

"Good day," Mr. Lennox bowed.

"It is nice to make your acquaintance," Aunt Gardiner replied after she released me from our warm embrace. "Mr. Lennox, I do apologize that my husband was not here to greet you, but he is seeing to work in his factory."

"I admire such dedication to one's industry, so no offense is taken," Mr. Lennox responded.

"Naturally so. For as I understand it, you are an attorney."

"Yes, I am."

"And he is often grinding at the grindstone," I commented. "Even when he is not working, he is working."

"You flatter me," Mr. Lennox responded.

"I do nothing of the kind but speak as I find."

"You are fortunate, Mr. Lennox," Mary observed, "to be able to go into such a vocation. If the world had been kinder to my sex, I would have liked to have gone into law myself."

This bold declaration initially startled Mr. Lennox, who was not used to women displaying such ambition.

"My sister has always had a desire for more than is our lot," I explained.

When I spoke, Mr. Lennox had the ability to compose himself and form an answer.

"I daresay, Miss Mary, that you would have been quite accomplished at being a solicitor, if given the chance. Either way, it is nice to hear admiration for my profession. Yet, factory work is just as vital to society as any other trade. You supply the world with the necessities that it needs to function."

"I always have desired to be of use, but as Elizabeth has perhaps told you, I was trained to be a governess."

"Mr. Lennox," Aunt Gardiner cut in, "I know that you are all staying very briefly before you both board the train to Darkshire, but I was wondering if you would like a cup of coffee before you go?"

"Actually, I would like that, if you can forgive me drinking it rather quickly."

"I can forgive you."

Aunt Gardiner wrung the bell for coffee to be brought in and she invited Mr. Lennox to sit down. Being a man of manners, Mr. Lennox engaged with her in polite conversation, which was precisely what I needed.

Taking Mary's arm, I led her to the window on the other side of the sitting room, so that I could have a private word with her.

"Mary, you look tired," I noted.

"It's because... I am, Lizzy."

"You are overworked."

"It's not uncle's fault. He gives me ample days off. It is merely that—I am so busy that I don't have time to practice my music and when I try to read, I fall asleep from exhaustion."

I read the meaning behind her words. Mary's studies were everything to her, therefore, to have her lose the time that she spent in careful contemplation and emphasis on education it would put a strain on her nerves.

"I know this has been very hard for you. It is the product of our upbringing," I explained. "Even though we were raised to work, it didn't matter. We lived lives of leisure, and so we are not prepared for this."

"Yes. I used to prize myself for my desire to work. Out of all of us, I wanted this life, but now..." She looked away from me, forlorn. "Elizabeth, I have no life left in me sometimes. I don't know what to do."

"We were raised to be governesses or companions," I noted. "We didn't foresee working in a factory. Even if it's the best one."

"We didn't take into consideration that, when the time came, there would be so many governesses and companions on the market, that there would be a shortage of placements," Mary whispered. "We should be grateful, I know, because uncle gave me work, I know..."

"But as you say, we are not used to this," I said, "when I begin my work in the North, I will look out for prospects for you, I promise."

Mary looked out the window. "If there are any, they would get snatched up by any governess in the area."

"They won't if I speak to Mr. Bell. He has property in Milton, and I am likely to see him when I get there, eventually. When I do, he might know of some positions, and he might put in a good recommendation for you."

"If he does, have it be for Kitty first. I know that she must secretly despise working as a chambermaid at the hotel."

"Kitty can withstand the work there for longer, I daresay. She enjoys meeting new people. Also, would you like me to convey any letter to she and Jane when I reach Milton?"

"I was hoping that you would suggest it."

She reached into her pocket that was on her apron and produced two letters.

"Any word from Lydia?" I asked her.

"No," Mary said, surprised by my question. "I would have thought that she would have written to you."

"Well, like she said, married life would make her too busy to write letters to the family." I chuckled.

"What's amusing about that?" Mary asked.

"Just something that I recalled. Remember when Lydia once said that she wanted to be married before any of us?"

"Yes," Mary sighed. "Should I be upset that she got her wish?"

I raised an eyebrow, amused.

"That sounds close to jealousy. Well, behold Mary Bennet; the moral one has admitted to having a vice."

"I do not!"

"You do too. It is quite comical."

"Oh, dear lord," she groaned, rubbing her head.

"Never fear, I needed a laugh before going on the road. You supplied it."

"How can you be so lighthearted, in spite of everything?"

"Because mother and father would not have wanted me to spend my life in mourning. I will not disgrace their memory by always falling away from man, and into darkness."

Mary scratched the side of her face.

"I miss them. Is that not funny? I was never their favorite child. But I miss them all the same."

"As do I. They did love us, it's just that things are quite complicated—the way that we live now. True affection is not encouraged in the way that it is supposed to be. Like Uncle Gardiner said, Victorian values have not enhanced things, but made humanity a little colder to each other."

"He talks about better times that were before we were born."

"Yes. I want to believe that things were better than this, at some point. Besides, Uncle Gardiner wouldn't lie. The way that he talks, things must have been better once."

"Miss Bennet?" Mr. Lennox called to me. "I think it is time that we began our journey to Heston."

"Quite right," I responded, standing up. Looking around, I grew sorrowful. "Oh, how I do wish that I could stay."

"I wish that we had the means to provide for all five of you," Aunt Gardiner stated, kissing me on the cheek. "I really do wish so."

"I know," I assured her. "Truly, I do. Tell Uncle that I do wish that I could have seen him before I had left."

Aunt Gardiner assured me of such when they saw us to the chaise. Before Mr. Lennox offered me his hand to help me in, Mary grabbed my arm.

"I almost forgot," Mary voiced. "A week ago, we saw Mr. Darcy!"

When hearing his name, I froze. It was one thing for Edith to speak of him, but another thing entirely, to hear Mary mentioning seeing him.

Instinctively, I looked around the street, as if frightened that Mr. Darcy's shadow would rise up from around a corner and engulf me.

"You saw him?" I finally inquired. "When? And where?"

"Oh, when we were walking through the marketplaces. Mr. Darcy was by himself. He was riding along on his horse. It was strange seeing him without Mr. Bingley at his side. I had grown accustomed to seeing them side by side so often."

"Did...did you speak to him?"

"No. We weren't close enough to acknowledge each other."

I closed my eyes, relieved. If he didn't know that Mary was here, then he perhaps didn't know of my family's present circumstances. And, regarding our past, Mr. Darcy was the last person in the world who I wished to cast my eyes upon. By so doing, our presence would antagonize the other immensely.

I was certain that he despised me.

And while my anger towards him had subsided somewhat, it did not fully leave.

My trip to Milton in the North came at the perfect time, it seemed. Give me clouds of gray, smoke from chimneys—I could weather it all, provided that I was saved from the awkwardness of the man who left me in a constant state of being offended, and me save him from his broken heart—if I did indeed break it.

Giving my final farewells, Mr. Lennox and I closed the carriage door, and we were off, where we would travel to the railroad station and then the carriage would be sent back to Mrs. Shaw's house.

Out of the window, I watched Aunt Gardiner and Mary grow smaller until we turned a corner and they disappeared. Emotion swelled up within me, for god knows when I would see either of them again. After all, I was now a leaf along the winds of chance. My life was no longer my own to organize and plan.

"Who is Mr. Darcy?" Mr. Lennox asked me.

"What?" I asked, coming from out of my thoughts. "Forgive me, what did you say?"

"Your sister mentioned a Mr. Darcy? Who, pray tell, is that?"

Chapter 2

Men, Great & Small

Doubt! The defining emotional state that haunts us all eventually, and it rested in Mr. Darcy's mindset.

Now many days he would have to feel such doubt of his own resolve and self-awareness, and it ate away at his conviction, confidence, and comfort.

'How wrong I have been for so long,' he thought to himself, 'and what am I doing now? Is this a retreat? Or is it simply an escape? One is cowardice and the other is courage. Courage to recover. I shall overcome this heartbreak. I shall!'

There, in the confines of his chaise, he looked out the window and saw passersby walking either to work or for leisure. With that being the case, the scene altered from seeing individuals of gray clothing, dark eyes, and furrowed brows, with dirty shoes, to wealthy individuals with crisp collars, lovely and vibrant clothing.

How much the poor clashed with the wealthy! How like a wave of destitution that rose up and seemed to engulf the attractive flamboyance of the aristocracy.

He despised the sight of them all. For, in the country, there was freedom from such scenes, such extreme and ugly contrasts, of downtrodden characters who have faces covered in dirt. Yet, as irony would have it, his eyes looked past the other carriages, the omnibuses and he looked on a couple of chimney sweeps, walking by with the chimney brooms resting over their shoulders. Both sweeps were walking in the same direction of his carriage, and they were laughing. What did they have to laugh about? How shocking it must be!

After all, despite the conditions that they had to endure, and the soot on their faces, their eyes were alight with joy. They were not unhappy, not retreating, nor downtrodden from their lot. How much of a paradox they were; for they were in a completely different state to himself?

He had all the wealth in the world that they desired, the country seat to the largest home in Derbyshire, an estate that was approximately ten miles in size—but they were the joyous ones. They, in their broken state, their *state* of poverty, and they were content.

Leaning back on the cushions of his carriage, he saw an omnibus drive past his chaise.

The future!

When he was a child, all these things, from the bus to the station, did not exist. All around him was progress, of life moving forward at an unstoppable speed. How stagnant he felt. How locked into stasis, he was. A great flow of life, it was, that moved along, and for a moment he wondered if he would be able to progress along with it.

In that instant, he wondered if he would ever be able to move forward.

To walk.

To run.

To ride.

And feel the confidence that was once shaken from him, due to his own blindness. The very blindness that he doomed himself to.

'*Elizabeth Bennet...what have you done to me?*'

His chaise arrived in front of King's Cross Station and his footman opened the door for him.

"Thank you, Williams," Mr. Darcy said, disembarking. "Do you recall your instructions?"

"Aye, sir," Williams responded, "I return the chaise back to your townhouse, where the valet will oversee everything. Is he going to follow you to Milton, sir?"

"He will in less than a week. I do believe I can do without him for a while. Besides, it is always wise to allow your employees to be given a reprieve from their work. When you return, make sure that Jefferson understands and establishes Miss Darcy's plans. The townhouse is not to be closed at all."

"Very good, sir. He shall know, depend on that. I hope that you enjoy your visit with Mr. Thornton."

"Thank you, Williams. Good day."

Mr. Darcy took a few steps and his eyes widened as his gaze rested on the entirety of King's Cross Railway Station.

"What a piece of work is man," he whispered to himself.

All around him were fellow travelers, entering and leaving. Leaving and entering. It was as if the earth was moving under him, time was progressing around him, and everyone had a purpose. Everyone was moving forward. And he felt so distant from the rest of them, under the painful fear that he would never connect to another living soul again.

But he had to recover from his past heartache. For, in his eyes, what was a man without his self-assurance? His independence, and his inner strength?

To his surprise, he couldn't find it at Pemberley. That was the largest shock of all. Pemberley was the one place in all the world that he felt a refuge from any pains that he would experience from the outside world. After all, nothing could compare to home.

Therefore, how much of a blow it was to return to the rolling hills and green wood that surrounded his home and still feel a tremendous loss. The sanctuary that was once Pemberley now antagonized him, for its sweeping fields, its beautiful wood, its perfect structure, and its beautiful rooms all felt terribly empty. Something was missing. The vastness of the void haunted him, and he knew what caused it.

He had intended to return to Pemberley with a wife. A woman to share the beauties of his home, of his land, and of his life. And only one woman would do.

Suddenly, his attention was seized by two passing individuals. It was a handsome couple. By the way that they looked at each other, they must have been newly married. A new pairing of husband and wife carry themselves differently than ones who have been wed for years. This new bride was lovely, and like Elizabeth Bennet, she had dancing dark eyes and curly brown hair. Her husband was tall, like himself, and had a very strong face. And in their eyes was light—it was connection.

It felt as if he was being mocked. To see the future that one desired for oneself...but you see it in the scene of other people and not yourself.

The image sent a sharp pain through Darcy, cutting him to the quick. It was his tendency to not entertain any form of envy. But in one way, he was beginning to feel it very much.

Gathering his resolve, he entered the station, already having his ticket and his luggage being conveyed by porter, as he moved along the terminals.

When he did so, he found his spirit beginning to liven as he was caught up in all the bustle and spectacle that lay around him.

Soon, his train arrived, to convey him to Milton, in the North, and he embarked.

As the porters put his items in a private compartment, they noted his discomfort as he sat down.

"Alright, sir?" one of them asked.

Mr. Darcy did not respond initially, but then he acknowledged that it would be rude to say nothing.

"I am not accustomed to traveling by train," he acknowledged.

"It's always an adventure to me," he responded.

"Even when you work here? I've often found that people begin to lose the sense of pleasure when one of their joys turn into their profession?"

"Nay, sir. Trains represent the best in us."

"What makes you propose that theory?"

"It shows how much, despite everything, humanity really is moving forward. Besides, trains give you something."

"And what is that?"

"A destination. I've always found them to be jolly things."

"Come on, Dobson," the other porter said, smacking his hat against his friend's shoulder. "Let's not bore him."

"I was just being friendly, and such!" The first porter snapped, closing Mr. Darcy's compartment door, in the process.

Soon, the train was prepared, and Mr. Darcy felt the wheels turn underneath him. He saw the station roll away from them as they soon began to ride through London and into the country.

With every station they reached, Darcy felt himself release another anxiety—until his mind had no choice but to dwell on the past that he was trying to rise above...

Earlier that year...

His carriage had pulled up along Mrs. Shaw's house. When he was allowed entry, he was overjoyed that Elizabeth was all alone in the house. Edith, Mrs. Shaw, and Captain Lennox had gone to the dinner party that his aunt, Lady Catherine de Bourgh, had held at her townhouse. Elizabeth had remained behind, under the excuse of being ill. When Mr. Darcy had discovered this, he left the party immediately, traveled to Mrs. Shaw's home and seized his opportunity.

The doorman allowed him entry and he told the steward that he would remain in one of the back parlors. When he was told that Miss Elizabeth Bennet was in the house, he requested the steward to inform her that he wished to request her presence.

While he was alone in the parlor, he prepared himself. Pacing back and forth, he did all in his power to gather his resolve.

He imagined her there, in the room with him as he prepared himself for the most important decision in his life. In that moment, he considered the disinterested part that he played in elevating Elizabeth to a greater position in life, giving her his heart, his home, and his wealth. Thus, he was prepared to experience all forms of gratitude on her part.

Mr. Darcy was very much aware that, by doing so, he would have to take Elizabeth's four sisters under his care, but he was prepared for it—at last. He spent many months laboring under the possibility that her family was a necessary evil that he couldn't abide.

And then there was Mr. Bingley. This was the other weight that added to his woes. He had convinced Mr. Bingley to not propose marriage to Elizabeth's older sister, Jane. And now here he was, prepared to look the role of a hypocrite, and not follow his own advice.

When Bingley discovered this, he would feel so terribly upset and he wondered how his dearest friend would receive such news. Yet his love for Elizabeth Bennet had reached such a feverish pitch that he was willing to risk his friend's bitter feelings, as long as he seized his love of his by the hand.

He was startled from all his inner musings when the parlor door opened, and Elizabeth Bennet entered.

When seeing her, all his nerve gave way and he forgot everything that he was going to say! If he had undergone this kind of circumstance before, he would have known that this confusion was customary, for no amount of preparation could prepare him for the actual event.

"Forgive me," he managed to utter, "I hope that you are feeling better."

"I am, thank you," Elizabeth responded. Reading her expression, Mr. Darcy could see that her cheeks were red, and she was uncertain of how to look at him.

"She was waiting for me," Mr. Darcy uttered to himself. *She is expecting me to propose and now I must satisfy the state of anticipation that must be rising up within her. She anticipates you! She wants this just as much as you do.*

"Would you like to sit down?" she asked him. When doing so, he was startled, because once more, words escaped him. Darcy knew what to say, but it was as if his words were caught in his throat and refused to be released.

She sat down in a chair and Mr. Darcy obeyed.

"Mrs. Shaw and Miss Shaw told me that you were unwell," Mr. Darcy began. "My aunt, Lady Catherine, noted your absence."

"I have suffered under a headache. My presence would not be good company, I feared. One should not burden others with one's company when one is out of spirits."

"Or when one's health is indifferent."

"Quite so."

"Colonel Fitzwilliam informed me that you were unwell when he spoke to you earlier."

"Oh."

"He said that you both encountered each other in the park. He saw you walking and offered you his company."

"Your cousin is a very respectful man and contains congeniality."

"Yes, quite so, quite so."

For a couple minutes, they had sunk into silence.

At last, unable to withstand it, Mr. Darcy stood up and

walked over to the fireplace. As he stared into the fire, the flames hypnotized him. Entranced by the illumination, he felt his courage rising.

It was time. He could not falter now.

Turning around, he faced her. Elizabeth had been sitting there, looking at him with a surprised expression. His behavior was, altogether, so very perplexing. He loved her all the more, ready to put an end to her confusion.

Taking a couple steps toward her, he breathed in heavily and began the declaration that would change his life:

"In vain I have struggled. It will not do. My feelings will not be repressed. You must allow me to tell you how ardently I admire and love you."

Elizabeth's eyes widened, in a way that Mr. Darcy mistook for subdued excitement. Her cheeks turned redder, and her mouth fell slightly open.

"It has been a great deal of time since I have begun to feel a natural and passionate attachment to you, that has overcome all of my logical objections to such a match. Indeed, despite all the losses on my side that I may endure at aligning myself with marriage to such an inferior family as that of Longbourn, as well as establishing a connection that goes expressly against my family's intentions, my friends' recommendations, and I hardly need add, my own reasoning and logic. Despite all the ridicule I may endure by attaching myself to a quarter that will lead to me being censured for losing my rationality and dispatching of all logic. But it cannot be helped. All of this, I would willingly face, in the light of knowing that I have secured your hand. Therefore, I humbly request for you to return my affections and consent to being my wife."

The question hung in the air as Elizabeth looked down at her lap. Darcy was left to remain standing there, waiting for her to give her acceptance, and relieve his suffering.

Eventually, she raised up her head and opened her mouth.

This was the moment! The very moment that Mr. Darcy

had dreamed of but had withheld from himself for long enough! She would accept him. She would make him the happiest of men.

"In such cases as this," she uttered, "it is, I believe, the established mode to express a sense of obligation for the sentiments avowed, however unequally they may be returned. It is natural that obligation should be felt, and if I could *feel* gratitude, I would now thank you." Her eyes grew darker, and her voice became stronger. "But I cannot—I have never desired your good opinion, and you have certainly bestowed it most unwillingly. I am sorry to have occasioned pain to anyone. It has been most unconsciously done, however, and I hope will be of short duration. The feelings which, you tell me, have long prevented the acknowledgment of your regard, can have little difficulty in overcoming it after this explanation."

This was a refusal!

It could not be.

Mr. Darcy could scarcely believe it. In fact, for a brief moment, he rejected the idea of what he was hearing. Although, very soon, the truth began to dawn on him that she had refused him, and the feeling of rejection began to swell up in his mind, making him feel a great offense. Before he knew how to reason with himself, he felt his anger rise within him. Unable to control his expression, he was almost certain that his disappointment gave way.

To conceal it from her, he moved away from her and rested his arm on the mantelpiece again, looking into the fire.

The fire mocked him!

It was as if it showed that it was more powerful, more overawing, than him. It provoked him to a drastic action. After a minute that felt interminable, at last, he turned back to her.

"And this is all the reply which I am to have the honor of expecting!" he remarked. "I might, perhaps, wish to be informed why, with so little *endeavor* at civility, I am thus rejected. But it is of small importance."

"I might as well inquire," Elizabeth replied, standing up, "why with so evident a desire of offending and insulting me, you chose to tell me that you liked me against your will, against your reason, and even against your character? Was this not some excuse for incivility, if I *was* uncivil? But I have other provocations. You know I have. Had not my feelings decided against you —had they been indifferent, or had they even been favorable, do you think that any consideration would tempt me to accept the man who has been the means of ruining, perhaps forever, the happiness of a most beloved sister?"

Oh, dear lord!

She knew about how he had advised his friend, Mr. Bingley, to abandon his love for Elizabeth's older sister, Jane Bennet. This was knowledge that she should never have learned about! How could she have found out? This, naturally, overturned every argument that he was about to make.

"I have every reason in the world to think ill of you," she continued, "No motive can excuse the unjust and ungenerous part you acted *there*. You dare not, you cannot deny, that you have been the principal, if not the only means of dividing them from each other—of exposing one to the censure of the world for caprice and instability, and the other to its derision for disappointed hopes, and involving them both in misery of the acutest kind."

Elizabeth stared at him with indignation, awaiting an answer that Mr. Darcy was not prepared to give.

"Can you deny that you have done it?" she repeated. This urging of him to answer finally pushed him to the reply that she did not want to hear.

"I have no wish of denying that I did everything in my power to separate my friend from your sister," he replied, calmly, "or that I rejoice in my success. Towards *him* I have been kinder than towards myself."

Elizabeth's eyes widened in alarm and disdain.

"But it is not merely this affair," she continued, "on which my dislike is founded. Long before it had taken place my opinion of you was decided. Your character was unfolded in the recital which I received many months ago from Mr. Wickham. On this subject, what can you have to say? In what imaginary act of friendship can you here defend yourself? Or under what misrepresentation can you here impose upon others?"

Now this gave him the right to respond. This woman, the creature that he had held so much in his esteem, had allowed herself to be duped by the most nefarious man of his acquaintance.

"You take an eager interest in that gentleman's concerns," Darcy retaliated, heat rising in his cheeks.

"Who that knows what his misfortunes have been, can help feeling an interest in him?"

What lies had that man given Elizabeth? And how could she listen to him? She had to have been foolish.

"His misfortunes!" Darcy exclaimed, resentful. "Yes, his misfortunes have been great indeed."

"And of your infliction," Elizabeth professed, spirited. "You have reduced him to his present state of poverty—comparative poverty. You have withheld the advantages which you must know to have been designed for him. You have deprived the best years of his life of that independence which was no less his due than his desert. You have done all this! And yet you can treat the mention of his misfortune with contempt and ridicule."

Taking a step forward, his anger was at a feverish pitch. However, he now desired to put as much distance between him and herself.

"And this," Darcy cried, "is your opinion of me! This is the estimation in which you hold me! I thank you for explaining it so fully. My faults, according to this calculation, are heavy indeed! But perhaps," added he, stopping in his walk, and turning towards her, "these offenses might have been overlooked, had not your pride been hurt by my honest confession of the scruples that had long prevented my forming any serious design.

These bitter accusations might have been suppressed, had I, with greater policy, concealed my struggles, and flattered you into the belief of my being impelled by unqualified, unalloyed inclination; by reason, by reflection, by everything. But disguise of every sort is my abhorrence."

Elizabeth stood up and walked away to the other side of the room, with her back to him. Translating her behavior as a retreat, Darcy pursued her, walking up to her to carry his point across. At this point, he knew that he had lost and was entirely mistaken in her feelings toward him. Now, he was only concerned in wounding her as much as she wounded him. It would not be until later that he would realize that he had sought revenge.

"Nor am I ashamed of the feelings I related, he continued, "they were natural and just. Could you expect me to rejoice in the inferiority of your connections? To congratulate myself on the hope of relations, whose condition in life is so decidedly beneath my own?"

This declaration was enough for Elizabeth Bennet. Turning to him, her expression was venomous. Now Darcy had her where he wanted—only now, he realized that he did not want that at all.

"You are mistaken, Mr. Darcy, if you suppose that the mode of your declaration affected me in any other way, than as it spared me the concern which I might have felt in refusing you, had you behaved in a more gentlemanlike manner."

This comment felt as if he had received a slap in the face and his heart was stirred. Mr. Darcy blinked, and for a second, his power seemed to deflate.

"You could not have made the offer of your hand in any possible way that would have tempted me to accept it," Elizabeth continued. "From the very beginning—from the first moment, I may almost say—of my acquaintance with you, your manners, impressing me with the fullest belief of your arrogance, your conceit, and your selfish disdain of the feelings of others, were such as to form the groundwork of disapprobation on which succeeding events have built so immovable a dislike, and I had not known you a month before I felt that you were the last man in the world whom I could ever be prevailed on to marry."

He had no more words of retaliation. Her professions had disorientated him, to such an extent, that he had no more spirit left for argument. His energy was deflated, and his confidence was shattered.

"You have said quite enough, madam," he voiced, his tone hollow and disturbingly calm. "I perfectly comprehend your feelings and have now only to be ashamed of what my own have been. Forgive me for having taken up so much of your time and accept my best wishes for your health and happiness."

With alacrity, Darcy left Mrs. Shaw's house and rode to Grosvenor Square, back to his townhouse. When he arrived, he ordered his valet, Jefferson, to send a note of apology to his aunt, for why he suddenly left her party.

Once he gave the instruction, he went to his room and sat down, both free and confined by the silence he experienced.

She had rejected him.

His pride was affected.

His confidence was shattered.

And his heart was broken.

Mr. Darcy rose above his haunted memory and blinked. He was still on the train, headed to Milton. It had been months since that painful day. Since Darcy had not seen Elizabeth Bennet since that disastrous hour, he believed that he would overcome the pain that his heart had endured.

Yet Elizabeth haunted his mind and there was still a place for her in his heart.

However, this trip to the North would surely be the perfect

diversion for himself. After all, Elizabeth remained in the South. In the North, there was no chance of meeting her.

After an arduous journey, the train soon arrived in Milton and Mr. Darcy disembarked.

"Darcy!"

He turned to hearing his name being mentioned and his spirits lifted when he saw his old friend.

"Thornton," he uttered.

Mr. John Thornton, the master of the cotton factory, Marlborough Mills, had come to greet him.

Despite that both men were stern by nature, there was an unexpected smile that rose to their lips as they approached each other. The bonds of long-term friendship!

Both men shook hands when they saw each other, and therein was a bit of relief in their eyes.

"How long has it been?" Mr. Darcy asked.

"A year, old man."

"Who do you call old? Am I not three months your senior?"

"Three months is enough for me to put some gap in between us."

"And that gap marks wisdom. Three months older, three months wiser."

"You and I have the uncanny ability of starting our conversations right in the middle, as opposed to beginning at...the beginning."

"The effects of experience, I suppose," Mr. Darcy said as the porter carried his bags behind them. "Do you have a carriage?"

Mr. Thornton did not answer readily, and Mr. Darcy read in between his silence.

"Perhaps we can order a chaise when leaving the station?" Darcy asked, rhetorically.

"There are chaises at the ready, sirs," the porter said, behind them. "I shall be able to get one for you quickly."

"Thank you," Mr. Darcy responded.

Both men didn't speak again until they reached the hired

chaise, the porter placed the bags into the carriage, Darcy tipped him, and then both men were traveling to Marlborough Street.

"I prefer not to keep a carriage anymore," Thornton explained, "since I live on the same street as my factory, I hardly needed to ever use it. I still prefer to consider expenses—especially with a sister such as mine."

Darcy chuckled inwardly, remembering Mr. Thornton's family—especially Thornton's little sister.

"And how is Miss Thornton?"

Thornton rolled his eyes.

"Fanny is the same as always. I wouldn't be surprised if she still is quite taken with you. You won't let her chase you away, will you?"

"Never fear, Thornton," Darcy assured him, recalling his time spent with Miss Caroline Bingley when he was in her company at Netherfield Park. "I've spent the last few months with a friend whose sister began to feel an inclination towards me. Time has taught me to weather such company."

"And who would this family be?" Thornton asked, with a raised eyebrow.

Darcy didn't answer but looked out the window.

"You do not trust me?"

"It's not that, Thornton. It is simply not my right to tell. Come now, if your sister were the sister of any other man, would you want me to expose her name to anyone else, even in a private setting?"

"Very well," Thornton replied, casually, "I see the point of that view. Whatever her faults, Fanny is still my sister. I would not want to have her name passed around so carelessly."

"Precisely."

Mr. Thornton looked at Mr. Darcy curiously.

"What is it?" Darcy questioned him.

"I am glad to see you, Darcy. Make no mistake on that matter. However, what is the occasion? You have always despised the sight of factories."

"Did I ever give the impression that I despised what you do?" Darcy asked, realizing the opinion that he might have left.

Thornton looked out the window.

"I knew the world that you were raised in," Thornton said, by way of an answer, "I knew what to expect."

"Yes, well...things are different now."

"Different?" Mr. Thornton repeated, turning to Darcy. "What do you speak of?"

"It is only—John, have you ever had an overpowering moment? Something that made you doubt yourself and wonder at how you came to a certain point in your life?"

"You know that I have."

"Well, I suppose, I have found that place. And I dwell there."

"Mr. Darcy doubts?" Thornton asked, interested. "Now this is a surprising situation. We mortal men doubt ourselves, as we have no choice but to. However, I never thought it was a place where you would find yourself. Does that mean that you would be interested in touring Marlborough Mills one day?"

"I suppose that I would not be averse to it."

This change was overpowering to Mr. Thornton, who was used to his old friend not being interested in the manufacturing side of his life. In fact, long ago, Thornton had to accustom himself to the fact that irony brought Darcy and him together, and irony maintained their friendship and correspondence through the years. Despite that his friend usually did not bother to acquaint himself with manufacturers, their characters were so much alike that their qualities couldn't help but recommend them to each other.

"What has happened to you, Darcy?" Thornton pursued. "I do not mean to pry, and I admire this change in you, but I must know. Is this change organic, or was something brought on by an incident?"

Mr. Darcy breathed in heavily again.

"I am intruding on your emotions again," Thornton acknowledged.

"No, it is not that," Darcy assured him. "I appreciate your concern for my behavior."

"Something does appear to be troubling you. As you said, your confidence is shaken."

"It is. After a brief time, I will tell you, but for the moment, I need to adjust to what I am feeling. All I can tell you now, is that I needed to escape."

"Escape? So much so, that you came back to the North?"

"The North was far enough away. I needed time to recover."

"Recover?"

"Thornton, I have received a great shock," he replied, heavily. "I have been dealt a great blow, and it rocked the very foundations of my spirit. You know that... I have no great love for the dust, dankness, and smoke that overcomes Milton, but I need to..."

"Find a refuge for a little bit of time?"

"Yes. If you will have me."

"Of course, old friend."

Darcy smiled slightly.

"Whatever my feelings on Milton, I am happy to see you," Darcy assured him.

"I know. Never fear, I know how to read between the lines of your severity and see the affection underneath."

Darcy smiled slightly.

"Thank you, Thornton."

They rode on, and eventually arrived in front of Thornton's home.

———

"I was remiss in inquiring on how your mother was doing," Darcy acknowledged as he and Thornton dismounted from the chaise and four. Darcy paid the driver to wait for him, since he was remaining in a hotel for the duration. Thornton had invited him to stay at his home, but Darcy preferred to remain at a hotel, for the sake of maintaining his own autonomy. Thornton didn't object to this because he knew how important freedom was to Darcy.

"My mother is still the same," Thornton said as they both entered. "Tough as iron and still my foundation."

"You have a good mother."

"Correction, friend. I have a great mother."

"So did I."

Thornton looked at Darcy, sympathetic. "Appreciate her while she is here."

"Believe me, I do."

"Is that you, John?" called a woman's voice. She came down the stairs and Darcy saw that it was Mrs. Thornton, John's mother. Removing his hat, he bowed to her.

"Mrs. Thornton, it is a delight to see you once more."

"Mr. Darcy," she remarked, her voice hard, but sincere. "It is a pleasure to see you. You have been away from Milton for too long. John missed you this last year."

"Mother..."

"No, she is correct," Darcy acquiesced. "Mrs. Thornton, my apologies for not being the most conscientious companion. Milton air just does not agree with me."

"It is not his fault," Mr. Thornton said, kissing his mother's cheek. "Much of his life is spent in the South. Despite our desire to see him, he can never fully adapt to our Milton skies of smoke."

"If you all may accept my invitation to visit Pemberley," Darcy added, "then you would see why I would miss the green that is home. But I daresay, you would get bored in the matter of a week there."

"You know that we are too accustomed to urban living and industrial towns," Mrs. Thornton said. "A leopard cannot change his stripes. Or her stripes, as is my case. Either way, I am happy to see that my son's friend has found his way back to the North."

Darcy was internally happy. Mrs. Thornton was a woman who was of his own ilk.

"Brace yourself," Thornton warned Darcy, "it's time to face the lion's den."

"Better for me to meet Miss Thornton now than wait later," Darcy deduced. "She would be angry if I retreated. Then again, I never believed in retreats."

Mr. Darcy followed John Thornton into a back parlor. Through the door, Darcy heard Fanny Thornton's voice. It was as shrill as he remembered it being.

Thornton rolled his eyes and gave Darcy a look.

"I am ready," Darcy assured him.

They opened the door and the first thing that Darcy was met with was the sight of Fanny Thornton turning around and standing up eagerly.

"Mr. Darcy!"

"Miss Thornton," Mr. Darcy stated. "It is a pleasure to see you."

"Pleasure indeed, you wicked man!" she bellowed, coming up to him and offering him her hand. Remembering that he was in Milton, he recalled that shaking a woman's hand was proper. So, he did so while analyzing her form and figure. She had grown a few inches since he last saw her. Her figure was womanly, her blonde hair was styled in the proper fashion that suited her face and she had overcome the awkward stage where all her pimples had diminished.

"You are growing into a handsome woman," Mr. Darcy offered.

"Oh, now that is a proper compliment," Miss Thornton declared, "being in this house, I can go months before anyone says anything remotely pleasant to me."

"That is not true," Mr. Thornton objected, "Fanny, you exaggerate."

"I do nothing of the kind. You and mama have as smoky a disposition as the skies themselves here. And Mr. Darcy, you finally arrive—and at the time where I have a guest."

She gestured to the other side of the room. Both men turned and Darcy's eyes widened, alarmed. His face froze, filled with horror.

"Miss Bennet," Mr. Thornton said, happily going up to her and shaking her hand. "I didn't know that you were coming to visit today."

"My apologies if I took you by surprise, Mr. Thornton," she responded.

"Not at all, not at all."

"Mr. Darcy," she said, turning to him. "It is a pleasure to see you once again. Who would have known that we would meet in the most unlikely of places?"

"Indeed," he managed to utter. "It is a surprise."

"You both know each other?" Fanny Thornton questioned, amazed.

"Yes," she explained, "I had the good fortune to meet Mr. Darcy when he came to Hertfordshire and was our neighbor for a time."

"Miss Bennet," Mr. Darcy said, bowing to her, "it is a surprise to see you again."

There, before him, stood Miss Jane Bennet.

The last woman in the world that he expected to see.

Chapter 3

Hearings of Heartbreak in Heston

T he train arrived in the railway of Heston, and Mr. Lennox and I departed it.

"There is not much to Heston," Mr. Lennox explained to me, "it is just one long straggling street that runs parallel to the seashore."

"Be careful, Mr. Lennox," I said, "or I would think that you are an enemy of the sea."

"It might be because I am. For some reason, I have never inherited the love for water and sand the way that other people do. Give me the dirt of London streets and the grind and grindstone of industrial images."

"I was raised to be a creature of nature," I replied, "and so a creature of nature I will be."

As a porter followed us with our luggage (which was not much, because we also carried our own), we disembarked, and I hoped to meet the faces of friendly people.

"Elizabeth!"

I turned to where my name was called, and further down the railway branch, was my friend, Margaret Hale. Putting my bags down, I raced up to her and folded my arms around her.

Surprised by this, she hesitated before she placed her arms around me as well. This led to me laughing.

"Still very reserved, I see?"

"You understand me very well," she said as we released each other, "it is just my way. Oh, Elizabeth, I am happy to see you."

"You very much had better be," I assured her.

She looked behind me and her expressions ran from extreme to extreme. First, she had suffered a great shock. Next, it was familiarity. I turned to where she was looking, and it was at Mr. Lennox.

"Mr. Lennox," she remarked as he tipped his hat to her.

"Miss Margaret," he said.

"I'm sorry. I did not expect you."

"When I discovered that Miss Bennet was coming to join you in Heston, I thought it fitting to be her chaperone. I am only here for a mere couple of hours before I take another train on to Sunderland, to visit a client who requested my presence."

"Even the North has urged you to leave the comforts of town," Margaret responded. Her tone was careful, and her words were even. Looking between them both, I got the sense that there was something I was unaware of.

"Yes, it has. You are looking very well, Miss Margaret. The seaside does you good."

"I thank you. I freely admit that I have found a new love for the sea." Margaret picked up one of my bags, I picked up another and Mr. Lennox carried my third, as we walked to the hotel.

As we walked, I looked out and saw the sea crashing across the sand in the distance, and I immediately wished that I could go and see it on a closer inspection.

"I am sure that you will like it here," Margaret assured me, "I cannot wait to take you along the crashing of the waves."

"It is a pity that the weather is not warm enough for sea-bathing," Mr. Lennox said. "With such handsome young ladies, I daresay that nothing could be more agreeable."

"Still an enemy of the sea?" I asked.

"Still," he confirmed.

When we reached the hotel, Margaret took me up to the room that her father rented and soon I was reunited with her mother and father, Reverend and Mrs. Hale.

"Reverend and Mrs. Hale." I greeted them warmly, and they smiled at me, in turn. When taking one look at Mrs. Hale, I felt that she was ill, in one form or another. Although, I never recalled Mrs. Hale being anything else but fragile in the whole time that I knew her. Therefore, perhaps I ought not to have been surprised. Yet she was a very kind woman, who suffered from nerves and disappointment, therefore, I had nothing against her.

"Elizabeth," Mrs. Hale professed, kissing me on the cheek. "It is a delight to see you."

"We were told that you are coming to Milton with us," Reverend Hale said, "and good afternoon, Mr. Lennox."

"Yes, I am," I replied, soberly. "Now that my sisters and I have to make our way in the world, it is best not to avoid our fate of finding a profession. But rather, it was my time to walk up to it."

"Oh, yes," Mrs. Hale said, covering her mouth with her hand. "I heard about your parents. You poor dear. To lose them both in a carriage accident!"

"Yes," I replied, trying to even out my breathing, so that I wouldn't cry. "It was very hard...it was..."

When sensing that I had no words for how I felt, Margaret grabbed my hand and held it. This bit of affection warmed me.

"Well," Reverend Hale said, "I prayed for your family when I heard the news. The only solace I can suffice is that Margaret has gained you as a companion. I hope that we will be family enough for you."

"That is a great kindness, Reverend," I cajoled, "I would like that."

"Oh, I suppose that my title must be changed. I fear that it is not Reverend Hale anymore, but only Mr. Hale."

"Of course," I rushed out, recalling that he relinquished his title as reverend, giving up his livelihood and coming to Milton to become a professor. "Forgive me, it is merely a habit."

"No apologies are necessary; that is what you are used to labelling me as."

We all sat down to coffee and refreshment.

In the brief time that Mr. Lennox stayed with us, Margaret spoke with him as little as possible. When watching them, I had time to analyze them both. More and more, I learned that there was something between them that went unspoken. It was an awkwardness that lurked underneath.

After a couple hours, Mr. Lennox took his leave of us to catch the train to Sunderland, and I was left to the Hales. Immediately, I wished to speak to Margaret alone, but it was proper to sit with the entire family.

I liked Mr. Hale, always had and always would. While Mrs. Hale was a nice woman, I couldn't ignore my memory of her. She was a woman who never found true contentment since I knew her. In any state that she was in, there was always something lacking.

She was born with the name Maria Beresford, and she was a lovely young woman, living in more cosmopolitan areas, in a comfortable home, where she could enjoy balls and parties quite often. Then she had the fate of falling in love with a clergyman of modest income. Both were madly in love with each other, despite that their lives, habits, and expectations were entirely different. Mrs. Hale was meant for a more affluent man of the world, and Mr. Hale needed to have a more practical wife, who had a sturdier disposition and was of more robust health. But alas. They fell in love with each other, and the rest was history. Miss Beresford became Mrs. Hale, she moved with her loyal servant, Dixon, to Helstone, a rural village in the South, and she didn't stop complaining about her life ever since.

Now, Mr. Hale was no longer to live there, but rather they were decamping and moving to the North. This did not deflate Mrs. Hale's complaints, but only augmented them. She was sad to leave London and move to Helstone, and now she was sad to leave Helstone and move to Milton.

This showed very soon after I arrived, and her words were supported by Dixon, her trusty and constant servant. Dixon was a large woman, who was Mrs. Hale's personal servant since Mrs. Hale was a very young woman. There was a bond between them that was stronger than iron.

"What say you to this all, Miss?" Dixon asked me, as an aside.

"To what, Dixon?" I asked.

"To this sad business of the master removing us from Helstone, abandoning his income and security, to decamp us to a cursed place in the North."

"Dixon," I whispered, "you know that I have no input on that matter. How would you feel if Mr. Hale heard you speaking like this?"

"I wish I could give him a piece of my mind, if it were only my place," she huffed, and then she went about her business.

At last, Margaret and I were able to have some time to ourselves. The first thing I did was give her the shawl that Edith offered as a present.

"Oh, Edith," Margaret said, holding up the shawl. "She knows that I don't need this where I am going—and it does nothing else but make me miss her." She wrapped the shawl around her shoulders. "She would make a fine lady of me yet. Yes, I miss her terribly."

Knowing that I was an active sort, Margaret offered to walk along the sea with me, since she knew that I was excited to do it.

"I wonder what it's like," I began, thinking of Mrs. Hale and Dixon, "to be a man married to a woman who has a constant servant as one's companion. It is as if Mr. Hale has married a woman, where there will always be another woman to crowd their intimacy." Margaret gave me a look. "I know what you are thinking. That I am overstepping my bounds and being too forward."

"I do not deny that you are correct," she acknowledged, "it would be foolish of me to ignore the veracity of that. Dixon loves my mother, but she doesn't always mind her words."

"But to be a husband where there will always be another person closer to your wife than yourself... I wonder what that is like? Then again, Mr. Hale is very patient. Perhaps more than I would be. Mind you, I do harbor a deep affection for Dixon. But I cannot help but observe things as I may."

"Still a studier of humanity, Elizabeth?"

I gave her a quizzical look.

"And you are not?"

She smiled slightly.

"I suppose both you and I are guilty of that habit."

"There's nothing to be guilty over."

I picked up a handful of sand and let it slip through my fingers.

"So, how have you all found Heston?"

"Oh, I love it," she answered. "When we arrived, we were glad to take the first clean, cheerful room that we met. For the first time in so many days I have felt at rest. There is a dreaminess in the rest, too, which makes it still more perfect and luxurious to repose in. The distant sea, lapping the sandy shore with measured sound, and seeing new scenes and new faces...it's helping me recover from the aches and pains that come from having to leave one's home and be so much uprooted from everything that one knows."

Realizing that she might not have been as empathetic to my situation, her expression changed to humility and sympathy.

"Elizabeth, I am so sorry. I am talking of myself and my own misfortunes when you are undergoing much worse."

"It is well to speak of yourself," I assured her. "You know that I am not made of such weak stuff that I cannot hear tell of another person's agonies. You and I both have been banished from our homes."

"My situation came from father choosing to leave Helstone, despite that he felt as if he might as well have been forced out. With you, you had no choice in the matter."

"You weren't given much of a choice either."

She looked ahead, toward the sea.

"I suppose you are right on that score. We both of us had to silence ourselves and do our duty. However, I still have my parents."

"And I do not. Yes, that is harder. I miss them every day."

"And father gave up our home. Whereas, with you, Mr. Collins couldn't help but return with a vengeance in his heart and...he dared call himself a clergyman! Men like him perhaps are the reason that my father wanted independence."

"Yes, we all want freedom, in one form or another."

"That's why I cannot despise my father. I cannot deny understanding the need to be able to order one's own life."

"I understand that as well. I do not deny hating Mr. Collins when he drove us from our home. Perhaps, I still do, in my heart. I forget—did I ever write to you about how he proposed to Charlotte Lucas after his failed proposal to me?"

Margaret's head shot around, surprised.

"He did?"

"Yes, he did."

"But, from the way that you write, you didn't tell me that she got married."

"Because she didn't. Out of respect for me, she politely declined the offer."

"She did? That was noble of her."

"Noble indeed. Charlotte didn't wish to hurt me, so she was willing to risk her future instead. I am beholden to her, now more than ever."

"Did Sir William and Lady Lucas ever discover this?"

"Yes, they did. However, Lady Lucas is unlike how mama was; she didn't torment Charlotte night and day on the matter. She was initially upset, but eventually accepted Charlotte's reasons and, of course, Sir William eventually held no disdain for his eldest daughter. I just..."

"What?"

"It's hard knowing that your friend might forever be single, because of loyalty for you. And to add to all that, she is loyal to a woman who was forced to leave the county when her cousin moved into Longbourn with his bride."

"If you and Charlotte Lucas rejected Mr. Collins, then who did he wed?"

"A Miss Letitia Morgan. She was one of his parishioners in Hunsford. Two weeks after our parents died, Mr. Collins wrote to us to inform us of him and his wife's arrival in a month's time. Once they got there, they spent every day giving subtle hints of asking us when we were going to visit our other relatives. It became too much to be born eventually, so each of us relied on our experiences and inquired of work elsewhere. Lydia got married to the first officer who made her an offer, and now she follows her husband's regiment."

"Kitty works in Milton as a chambermaid and Jane is a governess?"

"Yes. Mary also has skills to be a governess, but she works in my uncle's factory."

"In Cheapside?"

"Yes, it is," I replied. "Mary was always the one who could lend herself to a profession the easiest. It's weighing her down now, but she will always endure. For the rest of us, it has been quite a transition. Excepting Lydia, who got the life that she wanted."

"You once wrote to me that Lydia used to wish to be the first one to get married. That way, she could usher you to all the balls as a chaperone."

"She got her wish," I smiled sadly. "But there may never be any balls to usher us to."

Margaret took my hand, empathetic.

"Dear Elizabeth. You all deserve better."

"Thank you. I suppose, in life, we are given everything and end it with losing everything. But I wish that if everything had to be taken away from us, it should be taken slowly. Not taken all at once."

"Yes. That would be the best. But life just couldn't help itself."

"By the way, I couldn't help but notice that you and Mr. Lennox were apprehensive on that score. Or was I mistaken?"

"Oh, you are not mistaken at all. We didn't part ways well."

"Did he say something untoward to you once?"

"A bit. He proposed marriage to me."

I stopped walking in my tracks.

"What!"

"Yes," Margaret confessed, "he proposed to me. And I rejected him. Like you with Mr. Collins, I am a jilter."

"Yes, we are," I acknowledged. "Would you be willing to tell me the entire story?"

"Only if you promise me that I will not have to repeat it again. You know that I do not care to talk much about romance."

"Cross my heart."

"Very well. Here's what happened..."

We walked on, with her telling me her story. Months ago, Mr. Lennox had traveled to Helstone, specifically to propose marriage to her. She refused him, and they had been awkward ever since. *Fortunately*, Lennox was not her cousin who tried to remove her from her home. But it happened all the same. We walked on, each being a woman who rejected the proposal of a man.

––––––––––

In the short time that we remained in Heston, it was indeed heaven on earth. The seaside provided me with the very same peace that Margaret began to find there.

Even though Mr. and Mrs. Hale knew about all the tragedies that struck my family over the last five months, they still were willing to allow me to retell the tale of our misfortunes and offer me all the feelings of empathy that they could muster. I had no choice but to relive the loss of my parents, out loud. And they were patient in re-hearing it.

Being a true clergyman (though no longer one) who stood by the courage of his convictions, Mr. Hale's condolences for my cause were more heartfelt.

Mrs. Hale was wonderful, but it was evident that she sympathized with my tales of woe, because they matched her own. Often, she compared our fates because it justified her own state.

"I know how you feel, dear Elizabeth," she would say, patting my hand, "because it is how I felt when leaving Helstone for a place that I've heard horrible stories about. Our moving was decided without my feelings being considered. It was most unfair."

"But I recall you always not enjoying the weather or conditions in Helstone," I pointed out. "I thought this change would have been refreshing for you."

"It does not. One day, my dear, you will learn: the devil you know is better than the devil you don't."

On the last day that we were to remain by the sea, Margaret and I laid a blanket on the sand and watched the waves crashing against the shore.

How at peace we both were!

"I don't want to leave," she uttered. "I don't want to leave this place."

"Neither do I. For a time, it helped me forget about my mother and father being gone. This place has that much of a calming effect."

"But the future must be met, however stern and iron it be."

"We will persevere. We must promise ourselves that."

"Yes. We must."

"No matter what rocky shores we are dashed against, I am determined that we shall live." I gave her a side glance. "Do not make a liar out of me."

Margaret half-smiled.

On the day of departure, we were four in number. With our bags packed away in the compartment, we took the train to Milton.

As we did so, the sky began to change, and it was ominous.

Up ahead of us, we saw smoke in the skies, even more darkened as the Fall season began to reach its apex. Then we soon saw long, straight, hopeless streets of regularly built houses, all small and of brick. Here and there, were oblong-shaped factories, like a hen among her chickens, puffing out black unparliamentary smoke, and was the explanation for the clouds that we saw over the town.

At last, the train reached the railway station and we saw a view of Milton from the window.

"Dear lord," Mrs. Hale said, "this is worse than anything I imagined."

We all were silent for a brief time.

"Well, that's one way to greet a city," I professed.

Now we got our very first look at Milton, the industrial town to be our new home.

Chapter 4

A Great Shock

After we left the railway station, we traveled to the hotel where the Hales would remain. I stayed with them briefly, but then had to continue on, because I had come to live with Jane and Kitty.

Despite her being a governess, Jane was insistent on living with Kitty for a portion of each week, and they secured some small lodgings that was in Princeton, on Frances Street.

When I departed from the Hales, I finally was able to shamelessly look out of the chaise window to spy everything around me. This was easy to do, because the carriage had to stop frequently, due to traffic. The streets were larger and wider, but they were overcrowded with carts, wagons, omnibuses, and great-loaded lurries. Despite that I had visited the Gardiners and the Shaws in London quite often, this was still a new experience.

Everything around me was different! The heavy lumbering vehicles seemed various in their purposes, and intent. Every wagon, truck and van seemed to bear cotton, either in the raw shape in bags, or the woven shape in bales of calico.

Soon, we rode down High Street, which naturally was a main street that I believed I would frequent often.

Despite the apprehension of living in the North, a place that I was completely foreign to, there was a sense of exhilaration to it. After all, I was never afraid of difference. I was only ever afraid of having the wind knocked out of my confidence.

Naturally, one takes in the level of fashion as well as in the architecture. The casual person was dressed according to their station level. Those who worked had clothing of grayer and browner colors. And those who were more affluent clearly wore the fashions of London.

The more we rode through the town, the more I was made aware of how far my family had fallen, once both our parents died. And there was one thing that overwhelmed me. Due to the smoke and the natural climate of English weather, the principal color of Milton was *gray*. From the factories to the skies, to the clothing that the workers wore, even to the feeling of their faces against the industrial setting. It was *gray*. While it was visually striking, at first, I was still from the South. And more importantly, I was raised in the rolling hills and green dales of the country. I was used to color, actually, being all around. Hertfordshire got dismal weather every now and again, of course. Yet, it still maintained the illumination of country living. There was beauty. Here... was there any beauty of any sort?

Then I considered what the Hales were experiencing. While they lived at a parsonage, our experiences were similar. We both lived in rural areas for a significant portion of our lives, and we had preferred that lifestyle.

Eventually, the chaise turned along a side street and I began to see that Frances Street was...an area of town where the working class lived. And not the laborers who lived in a bit of luxury that had bits of wealth dripping over the edges of their purse. Oh no. This was evidently the residences of people who worked for their entire lives and had little to show for it.

This was where I was to live? This was where Jane and Kitty resided?

In that moment, I wondered if perhaps Mary and Lydia had been correct all along. But no! I knew, very well, that I could not marry unless I were very much in love, which I was not. Nor was I likely to ever be so, at such a rate. And as to Mary, I was not meant to be a factory worker. Even though mother made certain that we all were experienced enough, it was just not my habit. To be sure, I knew that I would make poor work of it.

When the chaise pulled up in front of Three Frances Street, I stepped out of it, and was immediately met by a distinct smell. It nearly overpowered me, but I was not the sort who fainted from fumes, so I looked at the small lodgings that were before me. As I did so, a couple of men passed by me. Their jackets, hats, waistcoats, and trousers were all a dark gray color, and their shirts were dingy. Two of them were smoking a pipe and they looked over my figure without shame or pretense.

"Well, aren't you a right bonny face?" One of them asked.

"Aye, to look on ya!" another one of them said. "Light against the smoke."

"You must be related to the two beauties in that there house," the third said, gesturing to the house in front of me. "Another looker to tempt us all to dream, eh?"

I smiled bashfully and looked at the ground, feeling flushed. I was not accustomed to such blatant compliments. It made me very apprehensive. We all want compliments, but they can be so very overpowering sometimes. And other times, they are frightening.

I looked up at the window that was on the second floor, and I saw two faces rush to the window.

Jane and Kitty!

They both waved to me eagerly and then I saw Kitty's face disappear, followed by Jane. Being quicker of step and more active, Kitty ran down the steps to greet me first. Soon, the front door opened, and Kitty rushed out of it, followed by Jane.

"Elizabeth!" they cried.

Laughing, we all embraced each other warmly. Whatever the scene we found ourselves in, we were together. As such, we were home.

They helped me bring in all my luggage and I finally got to see the interior.

To my utter happiness, the interior did not match the exterior. The house was small—literally, when you entered, there was no vestibule, but you were immediately in the parlor, and the second room was the kitchen, with a very small room behind it, to use as the privy.

"It looks lovely in here," I commented. The floors had dark brown wood. There was a lovely table, in the middle of the room, with five chairs that we were able to steal from our home. All the chairs had been given cushions and chair covers on it to add to the comfort. There was a bouquet of flowers that were in the middle of the table. The kitchen had a good fireplace, beehive oven, food storage areas, counters for food preparation, and a pickling area. It was all well organized.

"Our parents may not have been able to give us much when they passed away," Jane explained, "but they gave us enough to help me ensure that we don't live in destitution. Father couldn't leave us much, but he left us just enough."

"And there is no need to worry over upstairs," Kitty informed me, "we did our best to make it equally as cozy. There is color everywhere. We live the gray outside, so we refused to live it on the inside."

"That is the dream that I was hoping to walk into," I noted as I removed my coat, scarf, and bonnet. "For a moment, I was worried that the lack of Milton's colors had taken you both over, and I would be met with gray from within."

When I stood before them, we looked each other over.

"You both look very well, and lovely," I noted.

"So do you," Jane replied eagerly. Indeed, I was happy to see them still have life, vitality, and bloom to them.

"Has it been very hard for you?" I asked as they began to make me some coffee. I let my bags remain on the floor for a moment, and they let me not tend to them, because I was just so eager to see them again and hear about their lives. "To be in this town."

"It was hard at first," Jane began, "oh, bless me. It was such a shock, wasn't it, Kitty?"

"Yes, it was," Kitty confirmed, boiling the water, "it felt like everything was happening at once, and it was overpowering. So very overpowering and intimidating. I thought I would never stop crying, for a time."

This comment surprised me.

"I didn't know that you were still downhearted."

"You speak as if I have no feeling," Kitty said, "Elizabeth, do not be so unkind so early into being here."

"Oh, you know what I meant," I said, swiping the air with my hand. I knew very well that she was not serious. "It is simply that, when our parents died, you were the best at enduring it."

"I believe it was shock," Jane informed me. "That's what I believe."

"Jane has a theory," Kitty informed me. "That when our parents died, I was so stunned that it was hard for me to process the emotion of it. Or perhaps it was denial. Perhaps, my brain did not accept that they were fully gone. But after a few months, it began to occur to me that they were, and then I really began to feel it."

"On our first week here, I found her weeping in her room every night," Jane told me.

"Jane!"

"I am happy that you underwent it, little one," Jane assured her, "that is why I tell Elizabeth. Besides, I do believe that she needs to know about it."

"Indeed, I do," I confirmed. "Kitty, you were suffering?"

"Yes," Kitty said, finishing making the coffee. "I suppose that I was. It just took me longer than the rest of you."

She poured us a cup and we all began to drink it.

"How are our Aunt and Uncle Gardiner?" Jane asked.

"They are doing very well. They, naturally, worry about you both being here."

"Never fear," Kitty asserted. "We have learned that one can live without a man in the house and be safe. Besides, we have so many neighbors here who are aware of us, and with there being an inn right across the street, there is not much danger. After all, how much can a criminal get away with if there are always people to come running when they hear a woman scream?"

"Yes, we have learned of the safety in numbers," Jane summed up. "Of course, they are Milton men and women, who have a different way of speaking, behaving and acting. But once you get used to their habits, you will find them charming."

"I like everyone here," Kitty confirmed. "They are not afraid to talk about things. I like people who talk, even if the talk is crude. Anything is better than awkward nothings. Also, you traveled with the Hales?"

"Yes, they are at the hotel. By any chance, is that the hotel that you work at?"

"Yes, it is." Kitty smiled happily. "Today is my day off, but tomorrow, when I work, I am sure to cross paths with them. Most of my employers have no qualms of me talking to the guests, as long as I keep to my hours and responsibilities."

"How is Mrs. Hale?" Jane asked. "I recall her being a delightful woman who is very delicate. How does she find Milton?"

"I worry that this town might be a little trying to her health," I observed. "I worry about her now. Although she does still have Mr. Hale and Margaret. They both can endure much. I know they will look after her, and of course, she still has Dixon."

"I had a feeling that she would," Kitty replied. "That woman is tied to Mrs. Hale as if she was her mother."

"Dixon is loyal and affectionate," Jane said, "those are fine qualities."

"Speaking of fine qualities," I remarked, "what of the family who employs you?"

"The Kirkpatricks?"

"Are they still a lovely family to work for?"

"Yes. Their three children can be a little spirited sometimes, but that is the way that children ought to be. And they are a very good sort, who are rising above the most trying age of childhood. Also, the Kirkpatricks always have me driven home in their chaise and four whenever I am to stay with them."

"Very kind of them!"

"Indeed, they are."

"And what about you, Kitty?"

"Whenever I leave the hotel, I am always walking home with other women and men who work there. Because of such, I never go home alone, but with a crowd."

"Come!" Jane said, grabbing my hand. "See what we did with the kitchen!"

"Very well," I replied, merry from being in their presence.

One should not compare what was to what is, or one will be set up for the grandest of disappointments!

Therefore, I was resolved to suppress all my expectations when looking at the kitchen that now belonged to us. It was inferior to the one that we had at Longbourn in every way. It was small, cramped and there was perhaps only room for two people to cook at once—and even then, they had to economize with the room that they took up.

However, it was clean and had all that one needed to prepare a meal, which was all that one could hope for. Therefore, I smiled and complimented my sisters on a job well done.

"When staying with the Gardiners and the Shaws," I

explained, "I took it upon myself to continue perfecting my cooking skills. Therefore, you need not worry about making meals again. I can do that."

"We expected that of you," Jane said. "You are not the sort to leaf and loaf about when duties need to be done."

"We were of the suspicion that you would wish to cook, because we know how you despise cleaning," Kitty said.

"Precisely!" I admitted. "I despise it to an excruciating degree. I will cook, but that is the extent of my contribution."

"Never fear," Jane said, "I purchase all the food and Kitty cleans everything. Our dowries pay for the rent."

"And our extra income is used for to put into our savings," Jane explained. "We have control over our account that we have safely set up at the bank."

"Have you?" I asked, raising an eyebrow. "We are all made of stronger stuff than anyone thought. Of that, we can boast much about, if not for our own fortune."

"It is Mr. Bell's doing," Kitty rushed out, taking a mango out and beginning to cut it.

"Is that a mango?" I asked, amazed.

"Yes, it is. We get mangos now. Fortunately, the markets get more imports here than we got in the country." She returned back to her original subject. "We really must thank Mr. Hale again for introducing us to Mr. Bell. Once we came to Milton, Mr. Bell helped us arrange our affairs at a bank that we could trust. Since it's the same bank that organize his accounts, we know that we are safe when it comes to our financial distribution and interest."

"We don't have much to spend by the way of pin money," Jane added, "because we wish to save as much to one day at least get lodgings in a better area of town."

"Aye," I said, "Mr. Bell must've wept when he realized that Frances Street was the best we could do. You and Kitty were always great favorites of his."

"You exaggerate," Jane inferred, "he treasured you the most. We were just respectable by association."

"Do you think Mr. Bell will visit soon?" Kitty asked eagerly. "I wish to see him again."

"Mr. Bell is a wealthy and independent Oxford academic," I pointed out. "The South is his oyster, and the rest of the world is a diversion. And from the little that I have seen of Milton, why would he want to visit such a place so often?"

"To be among friends," Jane stressed. "Mr. Bell is a lively man, and he is considerate of his acquaintances."

"But that's just the point. He is the sort of man that can make friends or buy them by way of his prestige. Will he choose friends who live in a happier situation and a happier place?"

"You don't like Milton, do you?" Kitty asked.

I sat down in our one, and ONLY, parlor. Rubbing my forehead, I felt the exhaustion of the truth rising up within me.

"How can I?" I asked. "How can I ever love living in such a place?"

After my declaration, Jane and Kitty gave each other an apprehensive look.

"Of course," I furthered, "there is the novelty of seeing a new place, but when that wears off, what else is there?"

"Elizabeth..." Jane began, but I cut in.

"No, none of that," I stated. "There is no need to look at me as a spooked animal. You both know that I am not made for ill-humor or low spirits. Therefore, come back to me in half an hour, and I will be a changed woman." Then I blinked. "Or fifteen seconds in this case."

I chuckled.

"Yes. This is our fate, and I will meet it with fortitude."

"Soon, you shall become accustomed to it," Kitty

augmented. "Personally, I find some excitement at being in such a bustling place."

"The activity will eventually rouse you and you will be curious over it," Jane said.

"Yes, I just might be. Well, Elizabeth Bennet has come to the North. May there be no more surprises. I shall unpack."

"We will help you."

"Before that..." I said, removing Mary's letters from my purse. "Mary says hello and that she is thinking of you both."

We all sat down and read Mary's letters, which expressed her life at the factory and her well-wishes.

Afterwards, they helped take my things upstairs and we soon found the room in disarray as I had to decide where to put my items. Despite that Jane was the eldest and deserved her own room, our bond naturally made her feel compelled to have us share. This left Kitty, to her surprise, the freedom of still having her own room, which suited her tastes.

"Tomorrow I will go to the hotel with you, Kitty," I said, "and call on the Hales. Margaret and Mr. Hale will be going house-hunting tomorrow. I said I would go with them."

"Did Mr. Bell help them with their selection?" Kitty asked as she pulled out two Indian shawls from my bag, put them on and twirled around as she looked at herself in the mirror.

"He did, but they also discovered some lodging options in the Milton Times." My brow furrowed as I tried to remember the name of the other gentleman who had proven to be of assistance. "There was another man who helped seek out proper residences for them. His name was Mr. Thornton, I believe."

"Oh, Mr. Thornton!" Jane said. "Mr. Darcy's friend?"

I stood up with alacrity. All sense of disbelief filled my senses, but at the same time, I felt as if my hearing was true.

"Mr. Darcy?" I gasped.

"Yes." Jane's cheeks became somewhat flushed. "Forgive us for not mentioning it before—after all, we knew that it would not be news that you would look forward to hearing. Mr.

Thornton and Mr. Darcy are acquaintances—and this is confirmed because Mr. Darcy has come to visit him."

My insides froze over—all physical sensation began to leave me under the weight of this sudden and disturbing revelation.

"Mr. Darcy is here in Milton?"

"Yes, he is."

Heaven help me!

Chapter 5

Pains & Fears

"Miss Elizabeth Bennet?" Mr. Darcy repeated, after hearing Fanny Thornton tell him the name. Since Fanny was friends with Jane Bennet, naturally they were in each other's confidence. While it is improper for any lady to divulge too much of their friend's information, Mr. Darcy knew that Fanny would easily make an exception for him. Despite it all, she and Caroline Bingley were very much two of a kind. When Fanny had finished telling him that Jane Bennet's sister, Miss Elizabeth Bennet, would be joining her in Milton, he wanted to know everything.

"Yes," Fanny said, eager to please Mr. Darcy. "But Miss Elizabeth is not to be a governess, like Jane, or a chambermaid, like Kitty. No, she is to be a notetaker."

"A notetaker?" Mr. Darcy asked, his brow turning sterner. "She is to work?"

"Well, of course, she is to work. After all, her parents are now dead, so all the sisters have to earn a living."

When hearing this, Darcy leaned back in his chair, in concerned contemplation. It was a great curiosity, and he must know everything.

"You seem desirous to learn everything there is to know

about these Bennet sisters, Mr. Darcy?" Fanny asked, getting a look in her eye as if she had smelled something rotten.

"When I remained in Hertfordshire for a time, I gathered a wider acquaintance with them."

"Well, one would not have considered it as such. When dear Jane was here before, you only spoke five short sentences with her before you made quite the hasty retreat."

"I did it out of a desire to be tactful. The surprise I received from her appearance rendered me somewhat perplexed. As a result, I had no notion of how to approach any subject. Therefore, Miss Thornton, I apply to you now."

He sat down on the opposite sofa in the Thornton's sitting room, with Mrs. Thornton sewing in another corner of the room, minding their conversation, but never interrupting it.

Seeing that Mr. Darcy saw her as an authority figure on this subject, Fanny rose to her full height, sat erect in her seat, and began to explain.

"Well, they belong to those old-fashioned homes that were entailed to the male line."

"Their estate was called Longbourn," Darcy clarified.

"Yes! Well, their parents died in a horrible carriage accident and that left their cousin, Mr. Collins, to inherit the estate. After all, he was the only eligible man in the family to gain their home. When he did so, he allowed the sisters to stay for a time, but it was everyday implied that they needed to seek their accommodations."

"He passively removed them from their own home."

"Precisely."

Mr. Darcy leaned back in his seat, with fire in his eyes. He recalled how Mr. Collins had danced with Elizabeth at Mr. Bingley's ball at Netherfield Park. In an act of romantic misplacement, Mr. Collins had secured Elizabeth's hand for the first two dances. Watching the scene with much inner disquiet, Darcy had to wait for an hour before he could ask Elizabeth Bennet again. The wait was a miserable time for him.

And the dance with Elizabeth itself proved to be the bitter-sweet kind. It did not satisfy him, but it also left him wanting more.

And now, that same cousin who doted on Elizabeth Bennet, for the sake of making her his wife, had now changed his objective, married another woman, and had turned the Bennet sisters out of their home soon after their parents had left them.

The whole incident made Darcy feel sick.

"Mr. Darcy?" Fanny asked, confused.

Mr. Darcy casually and sternly shifted his features and tried to return to a less potent expression.

"Forgive me, did I startle you?"

"Yes, for a moment," Fanny replied, with a penetrating look. Knowing that there was something that she was not being told, she wanted to know of it. "How much were you acquainted with this family?"

"There was a neighboring estate that was not far from theirs, Netherfield Park. My friend, Mr. Bingley, rented the establishment for a time and I visited him there. While I was a guest, Miss Bennet and Miss Elizabeth stayed there for a week. Miss Bennet was friends to Mr. Bingley's sister, and when she came to visit, she fell ill and had to stay there till she recovered. Anxious for her sister's health, Miss Elizabeth walked to Netherfield to tend to her."

"Walked? Oh, so the houses were very close."

"There was a three-mile distance between both estates."

Fanny's eyes widened.

"Three miles?"

"Yes."

Fanny's mouth fell open, in disbelief. Out of the corner of his eye, Mr. Darcy saw Mrs. Thornton lowering her sewing, curious about this Miss Elizabeth Bennet.

"Well," Fanny said, "I suppose that is what it must be like in country counties in the South. You must have been alarmed. A lady in London, or the ton, would not have done such a thing."

"No, they would not. Miss Elizabeth is known for being a great walker."

"When has there ever been an award for that?" Fanny laughed.

"Fanny!" Mrs. Thornton chastised her daughter. "Walking is beneficial exercise for some. I've walked further in my life, if I needed to. You would have Mr. Darcy think us to be frivolous creatures, so easily puffed about."

"Mrs. Thornton," Mr. Darcy responded, "I have been well-acquainted with your constitution. As a result, I would never think any such thing of you or your family."

"Kind words, sir."

"Thank you."

"Also, I must know," Mr. Darcy questioned casually, "where does Miss Bennet reside? Since I am acquainted with them, it is fitting that I pay my respects there."

Fanny gave her mother a look and they looked down at the floor.

"What is the matter?" he asked.

"They rent lodgings...at 321 Frances Street," Mrs. Thornton answered.

When hearing this, Mr. Darcy cracked his knuckles, quietly enraged.

"Frances Street," he echoed, his tone deep and hollow.

"Yes."

"By the Goulden Dragon Pub?"

"Yes."

Mr. Darcy stood up and walked to the window, staring out of it.

"Jane doesn't tell me everything about what her life was like before her parents died," Fanny elaborated, "however, I gathered that Longbourn was a lovely enough home."

"It was," Darcy replied, his voice intense, "it was a great deal larger than anything that could be found on Frances Street."

"Then that means that they have fallen far down in society."

"Yes, very far. They were raised as ladies, daughters of a man of landed gentry. All of that has been stripped from them."

"People have been known to rise again," Mrs. Thornton said.

"Men have been known to," Mr. Thornton said, re-entering, "with women, it is not so very simple."

"No, it is not," Mrs. Thornton confirmed.

"They have only the chance of marrying well," Fanny said. "Jane would have had a chance at it, but there may be no chance of marrying now. After all, she is now a governess."

"Governesses are not universally disliked, Fanny," Mr. Thornton responded, "any chance will always exist. Darcy, I have to be returning to my Mill."

"And, thus, concludes my visit," Mr. Darcy said, with such finality, that no one would dare persuade him to stay. "Thornton, I shall leave with you."

"Very well."

Mr. Darcy offered his farewells and departed with his friend.

As Darcy got to his carriage, he turned to Thornton, who immediately began to expound on his sister's attitude.

"Sometimes, I feel as if Fanny forgets that we were poor for the longest time. Our position in society comes from being self-made."

"But you and she are correct," Darcy acknowledged. "Most likely, the only way that the Bennet sisters can rise to the same position they were born into is if they marry well. If they even want to marry."

"I never met a woman who did not entertain the idea of matrimony."

"You and I have had very different experiences with women."

Darcy saw Marlborough Mills up ahead. His time with Thornton was ending, and he needed to know something before he rode away. After all, he owed Mr. Bingley this much.

"Thornton, I must ask you about the true meaning behind something that you once said."

"About what?"

"About Miss Jane Bennet. You came to her defense, declaring that her new profession did not imply that she was below being proposed to. I wish to know. Did you make that remark out of compassion and logic—or do you feel for her?"

"For Miss Bennet?"

"Yes."

Thornton chuckled.

"Darcy, you don't know me at all, it seems."

Mr. Darcy raised an eyebrow.

"Do I not?"

"No. If I were in love, I would think you would know it immediately."

"Would I? You and I have a habit of being very good at hiding what we feel."

"But for me, not in this case. That is the strange thing. Miss Bennet is a superior woman in every way, and yet—I do not feel anything. I ought to, but I don't."

Mr. Darcy sighed inwardly, relieved. The last thing he needed was for Mr. Thornton to fall in love with Jane, knowing that Mr. Bingley was still very much in love with her. After all, nothing could be worse than one friend falling in love with the past love of another.

"I understand your feelings," Darcy confirmed. "And I agree."

"So, you are not moved by her beauty either?"

"I mark her beauty, but I do not stir under it."

"I do not believe that love is something I will ever obtain, and my indifference to her beauty is confirmation of that. I do not think I will ever marry."

"I felt that way once."

"What happened?"

"Life."

The men walked to Marlborough Mills and Thornton had to go back to his duties.

"Do you wish to dine tomorrow night at the hotel?" Darcy asked.

"I cannot, unfortunately. Tomorrow will be spent between my mill and inquiring after lodgings for a new tenant. When I finish, I will want to return home and rest. But if you visit the Mill in the afternoon, at 12:15, then we can partake in a luncheon."

"Very well."

"Till tomorrow."

"Till tomorrow."

Both men parted.

Now that he was alone, Darcy walked back to his carriage and proceeded to the hotel. Everything that took place outside of the chaise was like a blur. The figures that walked to and fro lacked definition. The scenery was smeared. His thoughts, feelings and self-assurance were seized once more.

Frances Street!

That was where Miss Elizabeth Bennet would now live. He should have felt elated at this news. After all, if she had accepted him, then this would have never happened. He would have been able to save her and her sisters from destitution or having to earn their living. But no! She refused him and therefore, she suffered the bitter pill that was 'retribution.'

Despite the knowledge of justice being served, he felt no satisfaction. Rather, he only felt a deeper sorrow for the state of her present condition. Elizabeth deserved better than to live there.

"You are still in love with her, Darcy," he uttered to himself. "You have conquered nothing. And you probably never will recover from this. But I will tell myself that I will, rather. It is the only way to continue on."

Darcy made his way to the hotel he was to stay, had the grandest room preserved for himself and was left to peace and solitude.

Chapter 6

A Second Glance

The next day, I woke up early and joined Kitty as she prepared for work. Despite the state of Frances Street, Kitty made sure to always look prim, proper, and presentable in her chambermaid dress. I made us some eggs, bread, cheese, and we ate some pickled mangos before we departed. Together, we took the omnibus and we each got off near our destination. Kitty and I got off first, because the family that Jane employed under lived further in the depths of Milton.

Once we got off, we turned down a street and were met by a large rush of people who were obviously factory workers. We got caught in the rush and I felt as if I was fighting back a large current of a human wave. Kitty grabbed me, laughing, to keep me from falling over and getting trampled by the onslaught.

"Is it always like this?" I asked, holding onto my bonnet. I was more startled than I was upset by it. Kitty, on the other hand, was somewhat exhilarated.

"Yes, it is. They are on their way to work. It's easy to get caught up in their mission."

"You find it amusing."

"I can't explain it, but their frenzy helps me wake up. Besides, their chaos makes me appreciate things more."

"In what way?"

"I could never see myself working in a factory. I'm sure that if I did, I would swallow so much fluff that I would be dead within half a year. I seek my luck where I may."

"Luck?" I replied, arching my eyebrow. "I haven't seen that word attached to our name in quite a while. Oh well, it's good to know that it rests somewhere."

Eventually we reached the hotel and called on the Hales.

"Miss Kitty!" Mr. Hale called to her when we met them.

"Mr. Hale," Kitty replied, "we meet again after so long." She embraced Margaret and Mrs. Hale, who both were happy to see her. While Margaret was always closest to Jane and me, she still did enjoy Kitty's company. However, it was Mrs. Hale who doted on Kitty and favored her the most. Kitty's lively spirit and voluble ways was always the sort of characteristics that leant itself toward Mrs. Hale and Dixon.

"How have you both been?" Kitty asked. "And did you bring Dixon with you?"

"They did, indeed," Dixon replied, entering the parlor, "Miss Kitty!"

"Good ole' Dixon," Kitty said, kissing her on the cheek. "Still a rock?"

"I'm not a rock; I'm a boulder." Dixon looked Kitty over. "So, you really are a chambermaid?"

"Well, I hate working, I don't deny that. But I do find some amusement in it all. At a hotel, there are so many people to meet and tend to, that I am never bored or feel wanting in amusement. At home, whenever it rained severely, it felt as if we were always removed from the rest of humanity."

"I know the feeling, my dear," Mrs. Hale said, taking her arm in hers, "sometimes, when the weather was awful at Helstone, I felt as if the world was completely removed from me and as if I would never see another living soul outside of my window. But Kitty, how can you bear to live here? After seeing the beauties of the country and London?"

"I live and work here for one reason only," Kitty replied, coughing a bit, and covering her mouth with a handkerchief, "because I have no choice."

"And this place has given you a cough," Dixon observed.

"I've always had a cough," Kitty admitted. "It's been my ongoing friend from one month's end to another." She looked at Margaret and me. "Only one good thing has come from now being orphans; mama is not here to complain about how my coughing vexes her."

"She was annoyed by your coughing?" Margaret asked.

"Mama's patience could be tried by the strangest of things," I explained, "especially if she was already annoyed by something else beforehand."

"Oh, how you both speak about your mother!" Dixon gasped. "Don't go speaking meanly of your parents, god rest them, or it will come back to haunt you."

"They don't speak meanly of her, Dixon, but factual," Margaret explained. "I'm sure that they do miss her, for all her characteristics."

"True," I responded. "Dixon, our household could teach you the beauties of laughing to ward off sadness and despair. Levity is our chief way of recovery."

"Well," Dixon said, pinching my cheek, "I will not deny the sense in that. See? I am not against learning new perspectives, for all that people say."

"Dixon is very loyal to me," Mrs. Hale said, "thus she has a natural inclination to mothers."

"Anyone of common sense ought to," Margaret confirmed, "Dixon, your words are safe from us."

Kitty could not remain long in our company because she had to begin working. She left, to tend to cleaning rooms. When I saw her depart, I noticed that she fell in line with the other chambermaids with ease and walked away with them, engaged in friendly conversation and jokes.

"And to think," I said to Margaret, "I pitied Kitty when I discovered what she had become."

"And she doesn't feel that way," Margaret responded, watching Kitty's light step as she departed. "She seems as if she was made for understanding the virtue of working for one's money."

"Virtue?" I laughed. "We humans, by nature, enjoy what we excel at, with as much ease as we can. Work is a necessity, not a luxury. Even you are aware of it."

"Am I?"

I looked past her and at Mr. Hale.

"Mr. Hale," I said, "forgive me if I am mistaken, but when you find that you could not remain in your present position, and began to take life into your own hands, was there a sense of relief on that score?"

Mr. Hale stuttered for a moment.

"Never fear, Mr. Hale," I excused, "you do not have to answer that question. With such a query, it is hard to have words for an answer."

"That is just the thing, however," Mr. Hale responded, a little perturbed as he put on his coat, "I have the words, but was merely surprised at your suddenness and desire to care for how I feel. Come, I shall tell you all as we walk."

He bade farewell to Mrs. Hale and Dixon, and he, Margaret and I left to go house-hunting.

As we walked along the Milton streets, I tried to be attentive to the street names, while also being an avid listener to Mr. Hale's feelings.

"Miss Elizabeth," Mr. Hale began, "it was more than just me uprooting my family from Helstone to this industrious town for the sake of rebellion. There was a desire for liberty involved, but it was done also as a matter of conscience."

"You did not wish to swear to indoctrinations that you did not believe in," Margaret clarified.

"Precisely. I could not and would not do it. The new bishop treated us like children and ordered us to reaffirm our faith in the book of common prayer. I know that it must look like I decamped, under a formality. But I could not live with myself if I adhered to it for the rest of my life."

"Then you did want liberty," I determined, "the right to order your life. You preferred that freedom over the freedom that comes with a steady living, where the work would continue to be a drudgery."

"And how do you relate that to people not wishing to work?" Margaret challenged. "I await that connection. For Father goes from one profession to another."

"He has to charge for lessons when he teaches, yes," I determined, "but you always enjoyed teaching, did you not, Mr. Hale?"

"Yes, I do," Mr. Hale acknowledged, "I confess to looking forward to this new experience that faces me here. To bring education to this place—I cannot deny that it might be difficult, at first, but perhaps that will enhance the adventure of it."

"There, you see?" I said, triumphing over Margaret, "unless one does the vocation that gives them much pleasure, humanity would prefer to leaf and loaf as it wishes. That is the pain of having a profession, besides how society views it; finding work that you like—and that likes you in return. But if you can't find that sort of line of work...emotional chaos!"

Mr. Hale and Margaret chuckled as we walked along.

After seeing a couple of establishments, both of which deemed unsuitable, Margaret was eager for us to separate.

"Let us split up," she suggested, "Elizabeth and I will see this next house, and father, you can see the one on Hobson

Street. This way, we can see more homes in an economical time."

"Are you sure?" Mr. Hale asked her, with a raised eyebrow.

"We will be fine," Margaret assured him. "It's an economical plan. The more houses we see today, the sooner that we can get settled, and the less money we spend by staying longer at the hotel."

"True," he consented. Next, he got a protective look in his eye. "Are you sure that you can understand the directions?"

"If we get confused, we can ask someone," I added.

"Please, do not go on any side roads, and be very careful."

"We shall, Father," Margaret assured him. "We shall see you again when we return to the hotel."

"Very well."

Mr. Hale nodded and left in the other direction.

"Two women on a destination," I narrated as Margaret and I walked together, "in an industrial town where they have no familiarity with. How long do you think it shall be before we get lost?"

"Not long." Margaret smiled. "But I'm determined anyway."

"I know you are." I chuckled.

While she didn't laugh, her face was heavily amused.

We reached a second street and Margaret came to a revelation.

"Then again," she said, "now is not the time to be proud."

Following her lead, we went into a shop and asked for directions to the first street of the house we were to visit. The shop owner was kind, very good at explaining, and we were able to go to the next house with ease.

"Sadly, the rooms are too small, and mama would not like the view from the windows," Margaret whispered after the proprietor showed us around the place. "It's a pity because it works perfectly for our income. But still—I could not make her unhappy."

"Where mothers and fathers are involved, matters never are simple," I theorized.

"I would easily bet fifty pounds that they are saying the same thing about us," Margaret responded.

"I am certain that they are."

We turned onto High Street and began to walk down it.

"In Hampshire," Margaret confided in me, "Thirty pounds a year would have been enough for a roomy house and pleasant garden. But here, two sitting rooms and four bedrooms are unattainable!"

"The shocks of being in a new place. The change of currency content can be extreme."

"Yes, it can. I confess that I was not prepared for that, though I ought to have been. Or perhaps I am being too hard on my own ignorance."

"We all of us are hard on our ignorance, from time to time. That is why I prefer not to think about more than I may."

"How is your home on Frances Street?" she asked me. "Is it better than any that we have seen?"

I looked down at the ground.

"Jane and I have to share a bedroom."

"And here I was complaining about four bedrooms," Margaret responded, empathetic, "I am sorry, Elizabeth."

"You ought not to be," I assured her.

"But I do. One should not speak of one's bad fortune when their companion must view you as spoiled by comparison."

"If all of humanity did not complain about their lives, because of the comparison to others, the human race would lose the power of speech."

Margaret smiled slightly at me.

"You are determined to save me from my own insecurities. I daresay, we might be the only true friends that I have ever known."

"Truly?" I asked, with a raised eyebrow.

"Yes. Think on all the friendships that you have known. Have they ever been found in a disinterested sort of way?"

Suddenly, it began to rain slightly.

"Oh, dear!" I cried. "Well, nothing for it!"

Grabbing her hand, I ran toward the nearest overhang in front of a shop, and she allowed me to do so.

"Get yourselves in," the shop owner said when he saw the rain getting harder. Having seen us from the window, he came to invite us inside, to take refuge from the deluge. We accepted, thanking him as we entered. It turned out to be a music shop and we were able to look around.

"Still play?" Margaret asked me.

"A little," I responded.

"A little will always be more than me," Margaret admitted.

"Do I detect regret, all of a sudden?" I asked.

"No," she smiled gently, "and that is the wonder of it. With all my qualities, or lack thereof, I never regretted not being musical. Either way, my dancing abilities have not abandoned me, so I shall be content with that."

We separated as we looked around the shop, content to admire the spectacles that lay before us, in the form of paper and musical notes.

"If one cannot claim familiarity with music," I said to myself, "at least one can marvel at the beautiful image of notes on the page."

Since the sky had turned darker, under the shadow of rainclouds, and mixed with the smoke that came from the mills, the windows grew darker, and it was easier to see the reflection of images behind you.

Faces danced across the glass as customers moved behind me, separate from the scurrying figures that were rushing outside, to seek drier places.

However, behind me one face fell upon the glass. Rather than moving back and forth, shopping for the right sheet music, it just lingered there, motionless.

Not turning around, the slight reflection arrested me, for I could sense a familiarity about it. The figure moved closer behind me, and I was able to get a better view of the face.

The face!

How could it be? And so soon! I was not prepared. How horrible that it must be for me. For him! For us both.

"Good afternoon, Miss Bennet."

I turned around, my breath practically caught in my throat.

"Mr. Darcy." I sighed. "Good afternoon."

There, before me, was Mr. Darcy, the man whom I had rejected a proposal of marriage from months earlier.

Chapter 7

Overcoming the Awkward

The agony and the awkwardness of the moment!
It was enough to make us both fall down.
There he was, as tall as ever, his face still a set of fine lines that were marked by handsome but severe features. When seeing me, Mr. Darcy slowly lifted his arm, removed his hat, and bowed.

Doing my best to recover, I curtsied to him and did all in my power to look him in the face.

"It ought not to be such a surprise to see you," I began, "for I was told that you were here in Milton. And yet, it is such. A great surprise, though our encountering was logical."

"Logical, yes," he replied. "I also was informed of your coming, and I feel the shock of our sudden meeting as well."

"My sisters said they had seen you."

"It was the eldest Miss Bennet that informed me of your joining them here."

"Yes. We reside on Frances Street. I don't know the extent of what Jane has told you, but our parents have passed away."

"Yes, I heard. My condolences."

I raised an eyebrow.

"Condolences?"

"Yes."

"Oh," I sighed, smiling sadly, "those words."

"I beg your pardon?" he questioned.

"Forgive me, sir. But you must understand, when Mother and Father left this Earth, that's all that everyone said: 'my condolences.' It has reached the point where the words now feel so very hollow and pointless. Perhaps you can empathize. Think of when your parents were lost to you. And everyone simply said 'my condolences'...after the first three times, those seem like the flimsiest two words in existence. Would you believe those words after a while?"

"No, I would not. When I lost my parents, there was not enough words in the English language."

"Precisely. You understand me." For a brief moment, I felt humbled. The connection I had made between our losses was the first true emotional comparison that we had with each other. Whatever was our past, there was a magnitude to it.

"Now," I continued, "take that pain that you feel, remember it, and bring it to this very moment. Would the words 'my condolences' be enough after a while?"

"No, it would not."

"Of course, it would not. It would feel as if those *words* were mocking you, and you are supposed to take those *words*, swallow them, and then label them as heartfelt. But now that you and I both are orphans in this world—"

"Orphans?"

"Yes. We may not be children in the eyes of the world, but we were to them—to mothers and fathers, we are always children. Therefore, when they died, we did become orphans in their immortal eyes. So, when you became an orphan, what were the words that you felt, that you knew were within you, and that you wanted someone to say? If you are able, say them now."

Mr. Darcy opened his mouth, and then closed it again.

"I see," I replied, archly, but not serious.

"You must understand, you have so much put me on the spot at this moment. I need time to reflect."

"Never fear. I understand. I would recommend to not apply thought, but only feeling. Go on then and give it a try."

He blinked and then he began to speak.

"Whatever words that I can supply to the moment will do nothing. I can say a thousand words and they would mean nothing, because they cannot capture the feeling of being so very alone in the world, where you become parentless and dashed against the cruel feeling of your security being so much snatched from you. So, I am heartily sorry for your loss."

"Thank you," I whispered, very much affected. Whatever our history together, I could not deny the comfort of his words. "That was precisely what I was feeling. Or rather, what I am feeling. That was perfect."

"Your fate is harder than mine. I lost my parents separately, so I had time between the losses. However, with you, you five lost both your parents at the same time. It must have been very hard."

"Unfortunately, it still is. I feel as if all my protection has escaped me. But I promise you this: I will not allow this to break me. My courage rises with every attempt to intimidate me. Life is one of those attempts. Tragedy is the other. Let them both do their worst. I will fortify myself. Neither of them will break me."

"No," he affirmed. He didn't smile, but his eyes twinkled a little. "I suppose that they will not."

We were interrupted by Margaret Hale coming upon us.

"Elizabeth," she said, "the rain is coming to an end. I think we can continue on."

Sometimes another voice in the room is all that one needs to break a spell. I started, recalling myself as all the other occupants in the store came to me, like a swift sunrise over the horizon. For a moment, I forgot there was anyone else around Mr. Darcy and I, for all knowledge of them had quite faded away. Instead, it felt as if the room around us, the very wood that *supported* us in the floor, had all but dissolved and Darcy and I had materialized in another plateau of existence. The man had altogether unnerved me and made me quite forget everything else around me. Then again...he often had a way of doing so, despite our sordid history.

When seeing that she interrupted my conversation with Mr. Darcy, Margaret turned to him, and I felt it proper to begin the introductions.

"Mr. Darcy, this is my friend, Miss Margaret Hale. Margaret, this is an acquaintance of mine from when he once visited Hertfordshire, Mr. Fitzwilliam Darcy of Pemberley."

"Pemberley?" Margaret repeated, "Then this must be the gentleman from Derbyshire."

"Indeed, I am, madame," Mr. Darcy replied, his traditionally serious mien returning to his face, and his eyes were like stone. This did not unnerve Margaret; on the contrary, I think she would have thought it was nothing short of proper. "It is a pleasure to make your acquaintance."

"Thank you," Margaret replied. "Like ourselves, you spend a great deal of time in the South."

"Yes, I do. Most of the year, I live there. My house, in town, is on Grosvenor Street."

"Then do you find this place as strange and novel as we find it to be so?" I asked. Now that Margaret was there, I had recalled the proper way of how to speak to a gentleman. I just realized that I had begun the conversation in a perverse way. Although, I also had to acknowledge that I didn't regret it. Not one word. Not one line.

"I have familiarity and family on my side," he elaborated, "therein may be the difference between us. As I understand it, this is your first time coming to an industrial town in the North."

"It is for us both," I informed him. "And there is even a

larger difference between us. Since you reside in Derbyshire and London, you must be coming here to visit, unless I am mistaken."

"You are not to be mistaken."

"But Margaret and I come to stay."

"Yes," he said, his eyes turning more keenly to me. Then he shifted his gaze to Margaret. "But you as well, Miss Hale?"

"Yes, Mr. Darcy. In fact, you caught us just as we were going to Crampton to look at a house for my family."

"You both were house hunting together?" Mr. Darcy asked, scrutinizing us. "Quite alone?"

"We are not alone," I responded, teasingly amusing. "As you can see, we are two in number. I know that you can count."

"And I also can spell."

"That I can confirm, for a whole evening was once spent with a discussion on your penmanship," I augmented, recalling when Miss Bingley once boasted of his incredible skill at letter-writing. "But yes, we are two in number."

"Miss Hale, did you travel here to Milton with family?"

"Yes, with my father, mother, and a loyal servant. Her name is Dixon."

"Your father chooses not to assist you in the search?"

"He is. Realizing that it would be faster if we separated, we would see more houses."

"Ah."

Margaret looked at me, a little disconcerted by his abrupt ending of discussion. Truly, he looked at us both and had nothing to say. Having known Mr. Darcy, I was used to this sort of behavior by now, but Margaret was not. Therefore, when he simply stared at us, she felt the weight of his gaze and looked down towards the floor. Instead, I looked boldly at him, marveling at his desire to remain in my presence. Or rather, mine in his.

Months ago, you proposed to me, and I refused you. You also willingly admitted to separating my sister from your friend and showed no remorse over the matter. You mocked your offenses toward Mr. Wickham, and boldly declared that you viewed connection to my family as a degradation. And here we are? Why are we not avoiding each other, but doing the precise reverse?

"Well," I concluded, "you came to a music shop. Therefore, I gather you are buying music for your sister? Unless you never informed me that you play yourself."

"I do not play, therefore your first assumption is correct; Georgiana remains in London with her friends, and I am looking for something that I believe she will enjoy."

"Mr. Darcy has a little sister," I explained to Margaret, "Miss Georgiana Darcy, who I have often heard is a paragon of women."

"Oh, I have never met a paragon before," Margaret inferred.

"I have," Mr. Darcy said, turning his eye toward me. The very impression of it made my stomach sink down to the floor in alarm and surprise. Every inch of my skin was being stabbed by invisible needles that aroused sensations of apprehension in me. I was not a paragon, so it was impossible to live up to such an accolade. In fact, many compliments were hard to live up to. Just as many insults were difficult to rise up from. And yet, could Mr. Darcy really be thinking of me in so kind a way? After all this time, could he still feel something, despite our turbulent past? If so, it was only proper to acknowledge this, and respect him in some sort of way.

"If you can ever write to Mr. Bingley or the Colonel," I said, "please give them my regards and mind the downpour."

Margaret and I moved to leave, but Mr. Darcy followed us.

"Are you both to walk to Crampton?"

"Yes," Margaret responded, "we have been told that it is not so far from here."

"The rain has lessened, but it may increase again. Let me take you both in my carriage."

Margaret gave me an apprehensive look, and I knew that the correct thing to do was to answer for the both of us.

"That is very kind of you, Mr. Darcy. However, we would be uncomfortable about interrupting your plans. As you know, I have never enjoyed being an inconvenience to anyone. Margaret is the same way."

"Then you will have saved me from idleness," he pressed. "I have a day about nothing more than simply dining with a friend this evening. I would be happy to be of service."

Once more, Margaret gave me a look, but I couldn't read its meaning. To continue to deny Mr. Darcy would have been rude and, for some reason, I wasn't in the mood to hurt his feelings.

"Thank you," I replied, "we would be delighted."

"Excellent," he responded, bowing his head curtly.

Escorting us outside, his carriage was drawn, and he offered us his hand and helped us into it. The carriage was off, and we rode along. Mr. Darcy seemed to be unsure of how to speak, or perhaps had nothing to say. As a result, I leaned toward the window and looked at the town as we passed by everything. Margaret did the same thing, our eyes widened at the novelty of it.

"Strangers in a strange land, we are," I noted.

"With strange experiences that will soon come our way," Margaret added.

"How often have you come to Milton?" I asked Mr. Darcy.

"I have never counted the times," Mr. Darcy informed me, "however, I can definitely say that it has been at least ten."

"Ten times?" I asked, surprised at my ignorance to his character. "How long can a person be around someone for so long, and still know so little? I never would have seen you in such a setting."

"You once told me that you were trying to make out my character."

"I did say that. And it was so difficult to get on at all."

"Perhaps I was remiss in offering you more clarity into my nature."

"One must not weep over missed opportunities."

"No, that would be fruitless. And you both really would have walked this far?"

"Like myself, Margaret is a great walker."

"Elizabeth does me too much of a kindness," Margaret countered. "I do not know if I can call myself a great walker. But I do enjoy a good walk, that cannot be denied."

"Did Miss Elizabeth ever tell you of when she walked three miles to see Miss Bennet when she was ill?"

Margaret's eyes lit up with hearing this story.

"Oh, really? Well, I should not be surprised at all, because you are such a devoted sister. But where was Jane staying that you had to walk to her aid?"

"At Netherfield Park," I narrated, "it was an estate in Hertfordshire that was situated three miles from Longbourn. I told you this before, but not in enough detail. Here is the rest. It was rented out to a gentleman by the name of Bingley. He set himself up there with his two sisters, one of his sister's husbands, and Mr. Darcy."

"Bingley is a friend of mine," Mr. Darcy added.

"How is he?" I asked.

"He is well. He is at the time where friends are aplenty, and he visits them often."

"I could not be surprised. Mr. Bingley strikes everyone as a popular sort of man." Turning back to Margaret, I thought it best to elaborate more of our history together. "It was through Mr. Bingley's temporary residence in Hertfordshire that I made Mr. Darcy's acquaintance. While the family remained there, Miss Bingley favored Jane and invited her to stay. While she was there, Jane fell ill, so I walked three miles to tend to her." I turned to Mr. Darcy. "I always wondered what you must have thought when seeing me standing there, with my shoes and the bottom of my petticoat and gown covered in mud."

"It was noted."

"Ah. The things you must have commented on that score."

"I found your eyes to be brightened by the exercise."

Blushing, I looked down at my hands again and didn't say anything else for the remainder of the ride to the next house.

When we arrived, Mr. Darcy helped us down from the carriage.

"Thank you, Mr. Darcy," Margaret said, "we are obliged to you."

"It was my pleasure. Would you wish for me to escort you inside?"

"That would not be necessary, sir. You have done enough, and I do not wish to take more of your time. And, well, I prefer to analyze a house in my own time and speed. Elizabeth knows to wait for me, but I will not trouble a new acquaintance to stand in a house while I inspect everything."

"Very good, miss." Next, Mr. Darcy turned to me. "Miss Bennet, give my regards to your sisters."

"I shall, thank you. I enjoyed seeing you once more, and in good health."

With one last significant look towards me, he climbed in his carriage and departed. We watched the chaise drive down the lane until it disappeared.

"You lied," I said.

"What? Me?" Margaret asked.

"You never take long to inspect a house. You wanted him gone because you wanted to ask about him."

Margaret gave me a sly look.

"Elizabeth, I have no idea what you are talking about."

We walked into the house.

"But since you wish to talk of him, I am willing to listen," she continued.

"Argh!"

When we walked into the front parlor of the house, we were met by an overseer, who was surprised when meeting us. When looking at us, his eyes widened in slight alarm.

"Can I help you both?" he asked.

"Yes, you may," Margaret began, "my name is Margaret Hale. We are here to inspect the house, as future lodgers. This was arranged by my father's friend, Mr. Bell, who had already selected some options for us."

"You are Mr. Hale's daughter?"

"Yes, I am."

The overseer turned to me.

"And I am Elizabeth Bennet, her friend," I explained.

"But your father is not present?" the overseer asked Margaret.

"We have separated to view more houses at a quicker fashion, so I am acting on his behalf." Margaret looked around the room. "We may begin whenever you are ready, sir."

His eyes shifted back and forth between us, at a loss of what to do.

"You are not accustomed to dealing with young ladies, are you?" I asked, not out of a desire to offend, but simply to reveal what unnerved him so much. After all, the sooner we could identify his apprehension, the sooner that he could recover from it and continue to show us around the house.

"I..." he stuttered, "well, I..."

"You are not."

"No," he sighed, "I am not."

"Well," Margaret continued, "I trust that this prospect will not overpower you to the point where you cannot perform your office? Or does it?"

The overseer scratched his chin, trying to steady himself.

"Let us begin."

"Yes, sir," Margaret said, "that would be best for us all. For you, the sooner that you start, the sooner that we can leave. That seems to be what both sides of us prefer."

"I—I have clearly begun this tour on the wrong side of the situation," he acknowledged.

"Admitting it is the first step," I offered.

He began to lead us around the house. The wallpaper was not the most becoming, but the floors were sturdy, and the windows were solid. The rooms were smaller than the ones we had at Longbourn, but since Margaret was raised in a parsonage for a portion of her life, it would be an easy transition to make. Much easier than my having to transition to living on Frances Street, in Princeton.

As Margaret followed the overseer around the house, I followed behind them, but was not as attentive.

I had seen Mr. Darcy again!

The shock of coming upon him in such a way had altogether disassembled me.

Yet, I still did not regret my rejecting his offer. And yes, I was upset with him for how he treated Jane and Mr. Wickham, but I was not made to revel in contempt for too long. Therefore, despite that I had not forgiven him for anything—after all, he never apologized for any of it—I found myself willing to speak casually to him.

But it was something else. Often, my mind had wandered to him, but it was always with extreme dislike. This, however, was a very different perspective and outlook. I was curious about him. His image ran through the other images in my mind and always appeared in the forefront.

In one moment, I saw the faces of my parents.

I saw Longbourn.

I saw Lucas Lodge.

Charlotte.

Sir William and Lady Lucas.

My Aunt and Uncle Philips.

Netherfield Park.

And each time, Mr. Darcy's face appeared before all of them again, springing into life through my thoughts. Why did he remain there? At first, I thought it was the surprise of seeing him so suddenly. Because I now was a woman of profession and I lived in Princeton, I had always assumed that there was little chance of encountering him. As such, to see him so very soon, it had no choice but to disconcert me, somewhat, and force me to linger on the memory of every past moment that he and I had together.

The speed of the mind! The speed of memory!

At last, Margaret finished her tour.

"What are you offering for this house?" she asked the overseer, "what are the rates of rent? We've seen some houses already, so I wish to see how your rate compares to the other offers."

"That part of the arrangement will be discussed with your father."

"Why not to me? After all, I will report to him when I return."

"Well...as to that part of things, if your father is interested, I am sure that Mr. Thornton would want to speak of such matters with Mr. Hale. He ordered this of me."

"Then I shall have to appeal to him directly. Who is Mr. Thornton, precisely?"

"Well, he is Mr. Thornton."

"And what does that mean to strangers in a strange land?" I asked, a little at my wit's end. "You must entertain that our ignorance is no fault of ours."

"Yes, of course, begging your pardon. I fear that I am saying all the wrong things. You must understand, I am not used to this situation. I just... I prefer to do as I am told, for the sake of professionalism. Mr. Thornton is a manufacturer and magistrate of Milton. He is the owner of the cotton factory, Marlborough Mills."

"Cotton?" Margaret repeated. "Then that would indicate that he would be at this mill currently?"

"Well, yes. He oversees everything and works there every

weekday." The overseer's chest swelled up proudly. "Mr. Thornton is one of the best masters among the others in his line of work. He is worth his weight in gold, I reckon."

"Then he must be of sound abilities to be good at listening," Margaret pressed. "Lead me to his mill so that I can speak to him directly."

The overseer blinked.

"If you will not speak of financial arrangements with my friend and I," Margaret pressed, "then we shall not trouble you to distress yourself."

"Rather," I added, "we shall appeal to the direct source that has held your tongue."

The overseer only waited for a few seconds before he agreed to this.

We left the house and followed him through the streets, to Marlborough Mills.

Chapter 8

The Master of Marlborough Mills

t last, we turned a corner and it opened into a yard of bustling life, activity, workers walking to and fro, minding their work or minding themselves.

"This is the mill?" We gasped.

"Aye, it is," the overseer said, "this way, if you please. Mr. Thornton would be in the main part of the factory. Little happens in the factory that escapes his notice."

"He sounds like a hawk," I related. "I wouldn't be surprised if his nose was straight and sharp as a flint of stone."

"Come to think of it," he considered, "his nose is as such."

"Even I wonder at me being *that* correct."

"Before you notice his nose, you will notice his eyes. That's where the real hawk lies. Nose smells danger. But it's his eyes that see it before it even comes."

Margaret and I gave each other a look and I had to suppress my laughter. His overseer was enamored by his master. I had heard such arguments before.

When we entered the factory, the overseer took us to his office, where he was met by an assistant.

"Where is Mr. Thornton?" the overseer asked.

"He's in the spinner's hall," the assistant informed him.

"Call him here and tell him that it pertains to two ladies who wish to inquire about the residence in Crampton."

"Fine, sir."

The assistant left, with the overseer remaining with us.

"How long have you been working for Mr. Thornton?" I asked.

"Five happy years."

"You think very well of him."

"He is a strong man. You need to be with this line of work. Especially with workers who are always thinking away about how they shall organize their next set of strikes. The fools! Illiterate and unintelligent lot!"

Margaret and I looked at each other, uneasily.

"Strikes?" I repeated. "Have those occurred here?"

"They are the common nuisance for any master who runs a factory. Mind you, they often end the same way: disorganized and self-destructive. Soon, the soldiers come and disband them really quickly."

"Soldiers?" Margaret repeated. "They arrest these strikers?"

"That never does much good because they play the martyr act if you do that. Rather, more excessive influence is often used."

It was very evident what he meant and the harsh idea of it was alarming. Margaret and I did not respond after that. A worker entered, with a problem in another part of the factory. Excusing himself, the overseer left us alone.

"Happy that he is gone?" I asked.

"A little," Margaret admitted.

Soon the assistant returned.

"Mr. Thornton says that if any discussion of a solid sale on the house holds interest, he will discuss it with Mr. Hale when they meet."

"So, he will not come?" Margaret asked, with a slightly raised eyebrow.

"He is overseeing the spinners and weavers."

"Well, then that settles it, doesn't it?" I noted. "If he does not wish to come to us, then we shall go to him."

"Right," Margaret responded. "Please take us to the spinners and weavers' area."

"Miss?"

"If you please."

This frank plea was enough. The assistant proved not to be immovable and led us through the factory.

When we entered the main room, it was large, and fluff of cotton was everywhere in the air. It looked as if it was snowing down on the workers, who diligently were tending to the spinners' and weavers' machines. Due to the fluff of cotton, Margaret and I were soon coughing, for it had gotten into our throats. We dismissed this immediately, because we were both so very amazed by the spectacle before us.

I had spent time in my Uncle Gardiner's factory before, and it was most industrious. However, this was a different scene altogether. It was still a new experience, seeing the workers toiling away, with white bits of cotton floating in the air.

"Elizabeth," Margaret said, her voice higher than a whisper as her eyes widened, "look at this all."

"I know," I responded, "I know."

For her, it must have been altogether quite the novelty. She had never seen the like. Also, knowing Margaret's apprehensions to the Northern ways of industry, she might have viewed this scene of labor as oppressive toward the workers' energy.

"Come forward, miss," the assistant said, "Mr. Thornton is this way."

We moved down along the room, with the workers and cotton moving around us. The men were attentive to us, in the way that a man's eyes would be when looking upon a new and strange woman in their midst, but mostly we went ignored by those around us. As we moved slowly down the aisles, a man emerged from one of the rooms in the back, stumbling backwards before he fell on the floor.

This sudden and dramatic movement broke the spell that we felt as we had been gazing on all that was new to us, and we felt reality come rushing in. The man who had fallen appeared to be thin, in his mid-twenties, and wore the gray clothing of a laborer. It was even more startling when a well-dressed man rushed in, looming over the fallen man.

"What did I say, Custer!" the well-dressed man shouted. "Never come back here again!"

"Please, sir!" the worker cried, crawling backwards on the floor. "I didn't mean to do what I did, sir."

"That's always the excuse," the other man said, grabbing the penitent man by the shirt and raising his hand. Balling his fingers into a fist, he proceeded to punch the fallen one in the face.

"I tell you that you were gone and gone for good!"

He punched him again.

This all happened so quickly that I felt frozen in shock, but soon I remembered myself.

"Can't you stop this?" I begged the assistant.

"He deserves it," the assistant replied. "The Master is teaching him a proper lesson."

The Master? Then...that was Mr. Thornton?

"There's nothing proper about that!" Margaret responded. Without caring for the history of the situation, she moved forward. Following her, we rushed up to Mr. Thornton, and Margaret touched his arm, gently, but urgently.

"Please, sir, stop this!" she cried.

Mr. Thornton stopped striking the penitent man and looked down at the hand on his arm. His eyes traveled from her hand, up her arm and at last, his eyes rested on her face. For a second, I had assumed that his eyes were filled with wonder, but that was not the proper explanation of it. Whatever amazement that he experienced by Margaret, who had grabbed his arm, now wore off and it was replaced by a wrathful expression and a severity in his eyes. There was madness; there was rage! Worried that he might exude violence upon Margaret, I ran up and stood behind her.

"Who the devil are you?" Mr. Thornton spat. "And what are you doing here?"

"I came to speak to you about the price of an estate that you are organizing with my family," she rushed out, without even thinking. "My name is Margaret Hale."

Now that I saw that he was not going to exact any sort of vehemence on her, I leaned down and looked at the man who Mr. Thornton held in his grip.

"Sir," I protested, "you must let him go now."

"Don't tell me what I have to do or not do," he spat at me.

"Please do not speak to my friend in such a manner," Margaret defended me.

"This man is hurt," I added, "he could be very much harmed."

"He deserves it, and once more, don't order me in my own business. Go about your own!"

"Sir," Custer wailed, "I am sorry. I won't ignore my duties!"

"You've caused enough damage!"

Mr. Thornton struck the man again.

"Please, this violence is not necessary!" Margaret argued.

"Neither of you are supposed to be here! Watson!"

The overseer who had tended to us before, had now come rushing up to us.

"I am sorry, sir," he urged, "I left them with Edwards."

"Get them out of here!"

Watson turned to us.

"Missuses," Watson urged us, standing in between our persons and Mr. Thornton, blocking us with his arms. "Please, come with me."

"We cannot just stand here and—"

"You must, missuses'," he urged, "please."

"He won't kill him?" I extoled, "we can't just—"

"Custer will be fine. Please, I beg of you to follow me. Please!"

Seeing the desperate look in Watson's eyes, we felt compelled to obey, for his sake, if not for our own. Allowing ourselves to be escorted out of the mill, there was a change in everything.

First, all the workers were now looking on us in wonder and interest.

Second, the image of the mill, on the way out of it, was entirely different than how it looked when we entered it. Now the white fluff in the air felt ominous, the machinery sounded diabolical and the whole experience felt as if we were being expelled by an inferno of belligerence and severity.

Despite ourselves, we couldn't help but turn around and see Custer's fate. After delivering his last punch, Mr. Thornton moved away from Custer and had his assistant help Custer up to remove him from the mill.

When we left the main hall, I could not help but appeal to Watson, the overseer.

"You said that Custer deserved that punishment?" I asked him.

"Because he did."

"I cannot believe such," Margaret refuted.

"Believe it, miss. Custer kept making mistakes since he began working here. He didn't tend to the machinery properly and could have broken it, due to his lack of attention to it. Also, there were other workers who could have been harmed by his negligence. With how this mill runs, if one worker shirks his responsibilities, the whole set can suffer."

"But not that way," Margaret objected. "Not in that way."

"I take it that you don't want to listen to Mr. Thornton now?"

"I do not believe that either of us would wish to be in each other's presence," Margaret deduced.

"Well, seeing as how this meeting took a sour turn, I'll just have to do the duty myself," the overseer said. "The rent at Crampton will be twenty-five pounds a year. Mr. Thornton will speak with your father if he is interested."

"I don't believe that we may wish to live under such a man," Margaret pointed out, "but thank you."

We had left the mill entirely and now were standing outside, in the courtyard. The mill was surrounded by a gate, and Watson had escorted us there. Seeing how we had taken to the scene that had occurred, Watson rubbed his lips, nervous, and scratched his chin.

"You saw my master at a bad moment," he explained.

"Did we?" I asked, raising an eyebrow.

"Yes, you did," he pressed. "You must understand, he has to be hard, because when incompetence occurs here, it can be dangerous. Custer had proven to be an incompetent worker."

"He could have been dismissed quietly," Margaret pointed out.

"I say this," Watson said, with innocent firmness, "you caught him at a bad moment. And again, his line of work requires a man with a temper."

He bid us a good day and we were left at the gate, perplexed at what we had just experienced.

As we walked, our conversation focused solely on what we had just experienced.

"We cannot live there," Margaret urged me to believe, "for how can we rent lodgings that have to do with such a man as he?"

"I see the situation you are in," I sympathized with her. "From the little that I have seen, he is a frightful and belligerent man. His overseer is obviously speaking from a place of extreme prejudice and preference. This Mr. Thornton gives him income, therefore, he naturally must make excuses for his master's behavior. Although, I suppose it is only natural, and it is a form of loyalty. When you are the one giving a living to someone, they always have a sense of debt. I do not despise Watson, but his obsequiousness and natural blind attachment is something that I have seen in another individual that I do not like."

"And who is that?"

"My dreaded cousin, Mr. Collins."

"He is not worthy of Longbourn."

"No, Margaret, he very much is not. Now, let's talk about this horrid Mr. Thornton. For it brings a glow to my cheeks."

"You are jesting. That means that you are trying to make me feel better."

"Is it working?"

"I wish that it was, but it cannot. Still, thank you, either way."

We walked on, and once more Milton had not given a proper impression.

That night, I lay in bed, while Jane was on the other side of me.

As I lay there, in the darkness, all the memories of tragedy rushed back upon me, and I was forced to reflect on everything.

The death of our parents, so suddenly snatched from us!

The loss of Longbourn.

Mr. Collins coming in with his new wife to uproot us from our home.

Lydia's quick rushing into marriage.

Mary taking work in a factory.

Jane having to become a governess.

Kitty becoming a chambermaid.

Our first sight of Milton.

The gray of the skies that antagonized us all.

The smoke, the bustle, the downtrodden look on some of their faces.

To discover what Mr. Thornton was, and how he was customary of Milton Masters.

And Mr. Darcy was here! Mr. Darcy of Pemberley, who now knew everything about our misfortunes.

I could have born it all with fortitude, if the turn our lives had taken was known only to my family. But now, with its fundamental truths being laid bare at the feet of the wealthy man whose proposal I had rejected?

I felt so naked, so exposed to everything.

And it all came upon me so suddenly that all self-control left me.

Before I knew it, I was weeping. The emotion filled my eyes, and the sobs could not be contained.

I tried to keep it quiet, but it was impossible.

Soon after my lamentations began, I felt Jane's hand on my shoulder.

"Lizzy?"

"Don't mind me," I rushed out, "I am being foolish."

"No, you are not," she insisted, wrapping her arms around me, like a mother did with their frightened child. In her arms, I wept even harder. "It is well, Elizabeth. Do not be scared to cry."

"I can't help it," I uttered, my voice broken from the emotion that poured forth. "When I came here, I tried to put on a brave face. I always do. It never leaves me. But now, I can't. I just can't. We've lost everything, Jane. We've lost everything and I feel so forlorn, as if I am cracking from within and I don't know if I can carry on. When seeing this place, I felt as if we have fallen into a form of hell. And I don't see the light out of it. Now, more than ever, I am certain. I just don't know! What is happening to me? Why am I like this?"

"You are afraid that your strength and courage are leaving you, don't you?"

"Yes! I feel it, and I hate it."

"Elizabeth, my strong little sister, I will tell you a truth that you do not want to hear. You are weak now because you have no choice. So much has been taken from us, and it was not taken slowly. It was taken so swiftly away, and all our security was removed from us to the point where it blinded us. We had no choice but to crack from within."

Her voice calmed me down and while I was still pained, at least my cries ceased.

"You are not alone with how you feel," she urged me to believe. "When I first moved here, I wept every night. Especially on the nights that I had to remain at the Kirkpatrick's home. I felt as if I had been forced to leave paradise and make my way as a stranger in a strange land. Kitty was in despair as well, as you know. But like me, every day that we wake up, we put one foot in front of the other and we learn to walk again. Every day, we do this, and the pain lessens even more. I will not tell you that the pain will end eventually, because I don't think it is meant to. But I promise you this; you are not weak for crying. You are human. We are allowed to be so, no matter what this godforsaken world tells us to do otherwise."

"Jane?"

"Yes?"

"Keep telling me that from time to time."

"I will."

"Good. Because, by doing so, one day, I might believe it."

Eventually, I fell asleep.

Chapter 9

Two Men, Two Moments

Sitting in Mr. Thornton's study, drinking wine, Mr. Darcy asked to borrow a pen so that he could compose a letter. Since both men were friendly enough and never needed to stand on ceremony, Mr. Thornton allowed him to do so. Rather, he was perfectly content that Mr. Darcy's company was so easy to endure because the day had been a trial.

Despite that Thornton did not tell him all his woes, Mr. Darcy was able to detect that there was a problem with his friend for the whole of the evening.

"Who do you write the letter to?" Thornton asked.

"To my cousin, Colonel Fitzwilliam."

"Oh! How is the Colonel?"

"As he describes, he is alive and that is all that he needs to be fulfilled."

"The Colonel always had a way of looking for the sun, even when the smoke covered everything."

"Yes. Even when the London fog feels as if it has leapt from out of a Mrs. Radcliffe novel, he still finds a way to bring levity about it. He wrote to tell me that his regiment is coming here and will be camped at Milton."

This sparked Thornton's interest tremendously.

"Really? For how long?"

"He did not specify the duration of time that they would remain, but I do know that he will arrive in two weeks' time. I'm writing to inform him that I will stay here longer to receive him."

"How long will you stay at the hotel?"

"I am unsure. Even that is not fixed."

"I envy you now. I would like to be allowed to roam about the world, able to do things indefinitely."

"We are similar men and different men, Thornton. I can stand still—you can't. I think you would miss the industry that you would have to leave behind."

"I was born to a life of working, but that does not mean that I could not make another path."

"If you were given a rich house, extensive grounds, and a country estate..." Darcy inferred, looking squarely at Thornton, "would you be happy? No, really, Thornton, would you be?"

Thornton looked ahead, staring at the wall.

"I don't know," he admitted. "after all, you have proscribed to me that I am not the sort of man who can abide standing still."

"You proscribed yourself. I merely was the first one to say it out loud."

"Darcy..."

"Yes?"

"I wonder, if sometimes, I am the sort of man who rushes out to seek conflict."

"What do you refer to?"

"I should rephrase. Sometimes, the fight seems as important as the intent behind it."

Seeing that Thornton was lost in thought, with his dark brow furrowed and his eyes so severe that it even made Mr. Darcy wonder if he looked such a way himself, sometimes.

Lowering his pen, Darcy turned to his friend and gave him his undivided attention.

"Go on then," Mr. Darcy allowed.

"Go on?" Thornton repeated. "Go on with what?"

"With the problem that is troubling you. You didn't speak much at dinner, and I can read all the words between your silence."

Thornton rubbed his eyes.

"This day is lingering in my mind."

While hearing this, Darcy flinched, for the memory of Elizabeth Bennet danced across his thoughts. Assuming that his day went a great deal differently than Thornton's, he was prepared for the difference.

"Why so?"

"Today, I had to dismiss a worker. His name was Custer. First, he had been found smoking in the Sorting Room, and that was the first strike against him. But he grew tardier at tending to the machinery that is used to spin the cotton. By doing so, he could have hurt the machinery, and he wasn't attentive to the safety of other workers around him."

"I'm sorry. To dismiss a worker is always a great nuisance. At Pemberley, I've had to dismiss servants myself, and it is always altogether never something that becomes easier with time."

"This one was passionate—I lost my temper. The man would not leave, no matter how many times I ordered him to. Between that and my anger of him endangering others too often, I...it grew violent."

"You struck him?"

"Yes."

Mr. Darcy leaned back.

"I cannot pretend to be a little... unnerved. However, I understand that, here in the Northern industry, sometimes severity is required. The relationship between master and worker is a strenuous one, where nothing is entirely black and white. All is gray here. I will not judge you."

"Thank you. But she might."

"Who?"

"There was a woman, or women, I should say. When I felt

compelled to—exact punishment on Custer, two women had come to visit the Mill. They were dressed simply, but their clothes flattered them. They had a look of two very accomplished ladies, and they were both handsome."

"And they saw you strike Custer?"

"Yes. But it's more than that. They came upon me, so much by surprise, and they opposed me."

"In what way?"

"They demanded that I stop. They cried for me to stop. In my anger, I ordered them to leave. My tone was harsh."

"And you are curious about the first impression that you gave them?"

"Yes. If it were merely a passing acquaintance, perhaps I would not be so unnerved by it. But those eyes... the eyes of one of them. It is as if the image of her, and the touch of her hand on my arm, still lingers in my mind."

"She touched you?"

"She held my arm, to try to persuade me to desist in my belligerence. I have a temper, Darcy, you know this. But the man was a danger to the workers in the mill. I have seen laborers in mills die because of negligence. I cannot risk my workers' lives."

"I understand."

"Well, at the moment, my temper had seized me. But afterwards, when Custer had finally accepted his dismissal, I had time to regain my composure. I wish that they had not come upon me at the time, and that I had not spoken so harshly. And worse, I fear that perhaps I might see them again. One in particular, her eyes when she saw me shout at her, it...it still haunts me."

"Why did those women come to see you? Were they looking for work?"

"No. My overseer told me that one of them was house hunting, for she had moved here with her mother and father."

Hearing this, Darcy ignored his letter altogether and stood up slowly.

"House-hunting? By any chance, were they looking in Crampton?"

"My overseer told me so."

"Did they both have brown hair? Of similar height, handsome faces, and womanly figures? One wore a long blue coat and the other a purple one?"

Thornton's eyes narrowed as he remembered.

"Yes, they did. Darcy, do you know them?"

"The one in the blue coat is Miss Elizabeth Bennet, of Longbourn, Hertfordshire. And the one in the purple is Miss Margaret Hale, from Helstone, Hampshire. They are both from the South."

"Do you know both of these women, Darcy?"

"I know one extensively, but the second, I've only made the acquaintance of this very day."

Mr. Thornton looked ahead at the wall, deep in his own thoughts.

"Her eyes. Those damned accusing eyes of hers. I still see them. I cannot help but see them."

Eyes!

When hearing this, Darcy's blood ran cold. Elizabeth's eyes were the very thing that pierced his soul to the quick soon after they met. Could it be that Mr. Thornton had been easily affected by them as well? If so, then this would be most inconvenient. If Thornton despised Elizabeth, then Darcy would have to argue with his friend. Although, if he was beginning to feel a softness for her, an unexpected tenderness, then that would be infinitely worse. It would throw Darcy into a secret fit of possessiveness. Despite that Elizabeth had rejected him, it did not diminish his affection for her. In fact, seeing her again, had rekindled any hope that he might obtain in that score. Especially if he could find the ideal time to tell Elizabeth the truth about Mr. Wickham.

But if Thornton were to begin to feel for her! No, Darcy wouldn't have that. That would cause a great rift between them, and Darcy would fight.

"Eyes?" Darcy repeated. "Which one of them?"

"The one who grabbed my arm. You mentioned that Miss Bennet was the one who had the blue coat?"

Mr. Darcy swallowed.

"Yes... I did."

"Then it was not her. The woman who grabbed my arm, facing me with such intensity, must have been the other one. It must have been Miss Hale."

When hearing this, Darcy closed his eyes. Relief! All had been put to rights, with no inconvenience on his part. Thornton marked Elizabeth, but his mind didn't linger on her. Rather, he preferred the handsomeness of Miss Hale. Both women, in their own way, were equally as lovely, from their dark hair to their round faces and penetrating eyes. Since their minds each lingered on a different woman, Darcy felt his spirits lighten.

He was suffering under the habit of many people who loved but did not obtain: if he could not have her, at least he could have the comfort of knowing that she would not be attached to anyone else in the present.

"They come to stay, Thornton. The Hales, I refer to. They are here, because Mr. Hale, Miss Hale's father, has left the church to take up teaching here in Milton."

"A tutor?"

"Yes, he has a friend, I believe, named Mr. Bell."

"Mr. Bell? The same Mr. Bell who is my landlord?"

"I can assume as such. Mr. Hale seems to teach ecclesiastical architecture, as well as the classics. Greek, Roman, and other classic culture. From what Miss Hale described, he will have younger and older pupils."

"All the sorts of studies that you would have learned at Oxford?" Thornton asked.

"Yes, perhaps."

"All the things I was meant to learn," Thornton said, looking into the fire. "If father had not been swindled."

Darcy was silent, for he knew that Thornton had fallen back into his family history, and the father who let down the entire family. When this occurred, Darcy knew better than to interrupt, so he went back to composing his letter.

All the while, he felt lighter. Thornton did not pay particular attention to Elizabeth, but Margaret instead. This was well. For this way, he could still keep Elizabeth all to himself, in his mind.

Chapter 10

Women of Work

The next day, Jane and I waited for the omnibus, and we rode it to our places of work.

"There is no need to worry over my not coming home today," she explained. "I have an arrangement where I remain at the Kirkpatricks for four days a week, then I am allowed to go home for the other three."

"The Kirkpatricks are very understanding, thank goodness," I extoled, "usually, families want a governess to remain staying at the house *eight* days a week."

"Yes," Jane said, "no matter whatever other circumstances are happening in my life, I have at least been very fortunate in that way. It was Mr. Kirkpatrick's doing. When I explained my situation, he was very kind about it. And besides, Mrs. Kirkpatrick prefers to have some nights where she tends to her children, so that they feel a stronger connection to her than is usually the case."

"A mother and father who actually likes spending time with their children?" I asked, with a raised eyebrow, speaking in irony. "How deliciously unorthodox. Then it follows that we shall not see you till Sunday evening?" I asked.

"I know that you will be fine while I am gone," Jane assured me, "you have a habit of being the quickest of us to recover."

"You do me too much credit."

"When I first came here, I cried every night for three weeks. You mastered it in one. You will do well here."

It came time for her stop, I squeezed her arm affectionately and watched her as she disembarked. Without her for the next four days, it would be just Kitty and myself.

At last, I reached Granger Hall. I called for my stop, disembarked the omnibus and stood in front of the large building. Its steps lay before me, like a majestic bit of ominousness. Every aspect of it had an intimidating factor—then again, education can be an overpowering thing. Necessary. And when taught correctly, it's even enjoyable. Unfortunately, most instructors that I have seen were quite abysmal at their trade. Their tones were monotonous, their rhetoric redundant, and their behavior tyrannical. It was almost as if they were selfish with their knowledge and did not wish to share it with the very pupils that they were there to enlighten. Perhaps there was a bit of vanity involved in the matter, but who knows?

Suddenly, for reasons that I cannot fathom, Mr. Darcy's face flashed across my mind. More importantly, his tone and attitude struck me the hardest. From his cold demeanor to the way that he lorded his prestigious education over everyone's head, exposing all to his superior mind—for, as much as I wished to deny it, his mind was indeed... superior. For a second, I entertained the idea of him standing in front of a classroom, with children staring up at him, expectantly. It was an alarming thing to think about. Children would run away from him in fear.

Unless he was as he was when I last saw him here, in Milton. He had softened under the weight of my history with him. If that is the case, then he could be gentler, when he chose. So, would Mr. Darcy be a horrible professor...or would he have found a better way of being?

Dismissing his image from my mind, I raised up my skirts

and climbed the steps. When I entered, it was to find a man pacing back and forth, expectant, and nervous. He was stout, and his cheeks were a little red. With his blonde hair parted to the side, a few strands would escape as he wiped them away from his eyes. As he checked his watch, I made a deduction of who he might be.

"Mr. Hunnicutt?" I asked. The man lowered his watch and turned to me.

"Yes, can I help you, miss?" he asked.

"My name is Miss Elizabeth Bennet," I said, "I am the new notetaker for the Hall and I believe that I am expected."

"Yes, yes," he said, walking up to me merrily. Offering me his hand, I was flustered. When he saw me confused, he removed his hand and felt ashamed. "Oh, you are not accustomed to shaking a man's hand, are you?"

"No, I confess that I am not," I admitted, "I have shaken hands before, but still need a little time for it to be the common custom. Forgive me. Did I offend you?"

"No, I should have realized. Forgive my ignorance."

"I need a little time to learn Northern ways, I acknowledge. Therefore, perhaps we could meet each other halfway in that score."

"Yes, you are from the South."

"Yes. I was raised in Hertfordshire. I am prepared to learn fast, I assure you. However, I will need occasional correction. If I do something that is not to the Northern customs, you will not be offending me by informing me of such. Due to present circumstances, I would prefer to do everything in my power to maintain this position."

"Yes, I was informed of your family's situation," he said. "May we?" he asked, waving his hand toward the hall.

"With pleasure," I replied, and followed him.

"My condolences for the loss of your parents," Mr. Hunnicutt offered. Ah! There was that *word* again.

"Thank you. It has been months since they passed, but I do

not deny that the loss still affects me. It would be foolish to ignore the reality of it."

"And too right you should not," he assured me, "to ignore the pain of a loss is not healthy to the mind, I have often felt. Better to expose your own reflections to the truth, or recovery shall never be obtained."

"That is just what I think," I responded. "I think I might like working for you."

He chuckled at this and then he sighed.

"I regret to inform you that you are not working under my employment. I am merely your contact. The main professor who requested an official notetaker for the hall was a Mr. Virgil Hanley. He organizes the hall and he himself is a professor."

"What does he teach?" I asked.

"Industrial Evolution and Engineering."

"An interesting area of education."

"Oh, yes!"

"When do I report to him?" I asked, removing my gloves.

"Right now," he informed me, "right now."

We stopped in front of a door.

The door was of a mahogany oak. For some reason, the image of it cast a great weight upon my mind.

"Nervous?" Mr. Hunnicutt asked me.

I smiled.

"Somewhat. The fear of the unknown, you must understand."

"Oh, I understand."

"Also, did Mr. Bell write to you about my situation? He informed me that he had."

Mr. Hunnicutt looked down at me over his spectacles, knowingly.

"Oh, yes, dear lady."

"Well, here is where the truth will out!" I remarked. "There is no one here beside me, so I will have to do my best to convince Mr. Hanley that this is the best course. When I first saw you, and you smiled at me, I thought that you were the one that I would have to persuade. I thought that it would be easy to persuade you that I am qualified to remain here, but now, I do not know what is on the other side of this door."

"In your case, it will take some convincing," he informed me. "Mr. Hanley is not a harsh man, but his mind does tend toward the *traditional*. And who doesn't?"

"Yes. After all, who doesn't fear the word 'change'? I confess, that word even unnerved me for a time."

"I will say this, Miss Bennet. I do wish that *I was the one* who you had to convince. If it helps, I would not have debated the issue for a minute."

"Thank you. Oh well, best to get on with it."

"Yes."

Mr. Hunnicutt knocked on the door and a thunderous voice said 'enter.'

"He also has a strong voice," Mr. Hunnicutt described, "but he is known to change his tone when speaking to ladies."

"Is that true?" I asked.

"Actually, I have no notion."

His lie was well-meaning enough, and I was grateful. He opened the door for me, and I followed him inside.

I walked into a *traditional* office that belonged to a *traditional* Oxford Academic. But there was one thing added to it: papers and books everywhere and in disarray. There was a rustic beauty to the clutter. But that was the only warmth that was exuded from the room. Almost as if it was succumbing to the intellectual idea of grays, browns, blacks, and greens, being the ONLY colors that adhere to a professional man, the room was devoid of any other vibrancy.

Along the other side of the room was a small library that opened to another smaller compartment. I was able to see as much, because of the windows that disappeared around the corner.

"Mr. Hanley?" Mr. Hunnicutt called, "I have our newest employee here for your review."

From around the corner of the bookshelves, Mr. Hanley appeared. He was holding a stack of papers over a book, and there was a pen in his hand, with a small container of ink in between his fingers.

When seeing me, he halted.

"Employee?"

"Yes," I said, "Good day, Mr. Hanley." Stepping forward, I offered my hand to shake—yes, I would begin to learn already! "My name is Miss Elizabeth Bennet. Mr. Bell wrote to you of me being recommended for the appointment of Notetaker for Granger Hall."

At first, he merely looked at me. This gave me ample chance to look upon him and note his appearance. He was of a fairly good height, being around five foot nine, he had a lean countenance, medium brown hair and was perhaps in his late forties/fifties. His eyes were sharp and penetrating. He wore dark green trousers and waistcoat, a white shirt, and gray tie-kerchief. His sleeves were rolled up and I could tell that my seeing his bare forearms unnerved him.

"My hand is here, sir," I said, still letting it hang in the air. At last, he remembered himself. Setting his objects down on his desk, he went to take my hand before I retracted mine. This disconcerted him, but then he realized the culprit.

His hand had ink on the palm.

"My apologies," he stated. Taking his handkerchief from out of his pocket, he tried to wipe it down.

"There is no need for that," I urged him, so that we could continue, "we can begin, surely, without the clasping of hands."

"Yes, we can...well, yes, we can." Mr. Hanley looked past me and at Mr. Hunnicutt. "I am afraid that I do not understand..."

"She is the new Notetaker, sir," Mr. Hunnicutt elaborated.

Mr. Hanley turned to me, critical.

"There must be some mistake."

"Mr. Hunnicutt," I said, "thank you for escorting me to Mr. Hanley. You do not need to remain to see what happens next."

"Very good, dear lady," he said, "if you do need any more assistance, I shall be in the next office, to the right."

"Thank you, sir."

Mr. Hunnicutt left us. Mr. Hanley still looked at me in disbelief, but I was prepared for this.

"If you do not mind," I voiced, "I shall sit."

"Oh, yes...of course."

I sat down in the seat opposite him, unbuttoning my coat. While I did so, Mr. Hanley's eyes never left me. This did not intimidate me one jot! After all, I had been prepared for this the entire time. Therefore, my courage needed to not let me down.

Looking up at Mr. Hanley, I saw his eyes still looking on me with a cold criticalness.

"I suspect that you are surprised by who I am."

"Yes, I am," he replied. Walking to the other side of his desk, he sat down slowly in his chair. "I suspect that I ought to offer you some refreshment, but I have nothing on hand, I am afraid."

"I understand. I've come to gather all the information for my duties. From knowing when is the first day that I begin, what are the hours that I ought to come, the names of the professors that I am to assist, and what hours I am to keep per week. Also, I was informed that you would supply all the paper and ink for my services."

"Miss..."

"Bennet."

"Yes. I am sorry, there must be some kind of mistake during all the proceedings."

"I understand your confusion over the matter."

He leaned forward.

"Do you?"

"Yes. Mr. Bell informed me that I would go into this interview with you never being informed that I am a woman."

"Correct."

And the moment of confrontation arrived.

"Well," I gathered, "I suppose that the subject would be inevitable, therefore, yes, you may discuss it."

"Miss Bennet, I have been denied critical information."

"Critical?"

"Yes. I have been quite deceived."

"How so, sir? After all, Mr. Bell wrote that you would receive an experienced Notetaker by the name of E. Bennet. He has seen, firsthand, my diligence to my work and my improvement over the years."

"Improvement?" he asked, with a raised eyebrow.

"I do not deny that I was terrible when I first started. Or mediocre, if you will. However, I applied myself and have proven myself to be as reliable and dependable as anyone else in the amanuensis profession."

"I was not told that you were—"

"A woman."

"Precisely."

"Does this mean that you will not employ me? Despite my references, recommendations and the fact that I uprooted myself from London to Milton?"

"Well, you must understand..."

"That there is no room for consideration of my qualifications because of incorrect preferences."

"Incorrect preferences? I was misinformed that you were a woman."

"And what does that have to do with anything?"

"There is no such thing as female Notetakers."

"Correction. There is no such thing as female Notetakers *here* in Milton."

He raised an eyebrow again; he seemed to do that a lot.

"Are you about to inform me that there are other areas in London that are employing a female amanuensis in schools such as these?"

"Perhaps not in Cambridge or Oxford, but the idea of having a female Notetaker is beginning to come into fashion. And even if it doesn't, that is superfluous in my situation."

"And why so?"

"Because... Mr. Hanley, I was told that you have a fair-minded way about you. Or at the very least, that you have the ability to give someone a chance and allow them to prove themselves. Mr. Bell did not include my sex, because he did not think it mattered. Or at the very least, he would find our predicament amusing. Either way, he knew that when I presented myself, I would be given a chance."

He leaned back in his chair and rubbed his lip. There was no more reason to give, so I just waited for him to respond.

At last, he leaned forward in his chair.

"I will have to test you," he informed me.

"Provide me with a pen, paper and ink," I said, placing my reticule on the floor. "And a desk to begin, then we can start."

He flinched.

"You are a very determined young lady."

"I am a lady who has lost her parents and must make her own way in the world. I find that I prefer to earn my keep and holding up a pretense of delicacy gets nothing done. Therefore, we can begin this test whenever you are ready."

Not wasting any time, he produced the paper, pen and ink and let me sit at a small desk in the room. I placed a line down the page, so that I could write the information in columns.

"Ready?" he asked.

"Aye."

He began to give a lecture and I began to take the notes as he spoke.

———————

After fifteen minutes of this, he stopped and requested to see how I had fared.

"I wrote in shorthand, if you don't mind," I said, "I did so for the sake of accuracy, and have no qualms on re-writing things in full-phrasing. Would you like me to do that first?"

"A true Oxford Academic learns shorthand," he said, putting on his spectacles. Walking over to me, he grabbed the papers greedily and began to read it. Calmly, I sat there and waited. Whether he liked my notation or not, was entirely up to him. I had learned the trade to the best of my ability and my self-assurance would not be shaken over whatever he determined.

At last, he finished reading. Lowering the pages, he removed his spectacles, sat down at his desk, and cast his eyes upon me.

"Well?" I questioned. "What is to be my fate? After all, you're the one who determines it."

"You have a sharp tongue," he said, "you will have to correct that, if you are to work here."

"Why?"

"Because it is not professional."

"Have I used my words incorrectly?" I asked, sitting still and very much unintimidated.

"If you are to work here, I would require you to be civil."

"What is uncivil about my speech?"

"It is—"

"Free?"

When I uttered the word, he blinked.

"Mr. Hanley," I continued, keeping my voice even, "you must excuse me, but I've rarely met a proper man, or a poor man, who feared speaking to me. And for the few who did, and those are VERY few, they seemed to suffer under the weight of a deep insecurity. Most of the men that I've met were too secure to fear the depths that a voice like mine could raise. It was for this reason that Mr. Bell recommended me to you."

"Was it?"

"Yes. He believed that I could thrive here...because he knew that I could hold a conversation. And look anyone in the eye. Wouldn't you want someone like that for your notetaker? After all, these professors will need someone who makes them comfortable. Polite silence does not always conjure natural coexistence. Sir, please, tell me your reflections of my writing sample."

He leaned back in his chair again and looked at the paper.

"You captured all the main points of the argument, all the keywords, and there was perfect clarity to your sentences. Also, your penmanship is clear and easy to read, which is the main thing. But there is the other dilemma. Or rather, the last impediment."

"Impediment?"

"Yes. It was the main apprehension that first occurred to me when I saw you. Your gender's chief issue, for my part, is in the distracting element of it."

"Distracting?"

"You are a young woman. And, if you don't mind my saying so, but you are extremely handsome. To see a lady writing away while in the class might be distracting to the gentlemen pupils."

"I am not often described as being handsome."

"Then the standards of beauty must be very extreme in the South. Here in the North, a pretty face is all the same to any man." He stood up, went over to the window, and stared out of it. Easily, I began to understand that he was the sort of a man of such deep reflection, that any decision he made rose and fell after episodes of quiet deliberation.

"Miss Bennet, I am a practical man, and so I do this, as no sign of disrespect to you."

I breathed inwardly, feeling the apprehension of rejection

rise up and prepare to engulf me. Here came the bad news, and all my prospects would come crashing down before my feet. If I did not secure this position, where was I to turn? I would not be able to sustain myself and would be but a lump of baggage that Kitty and Jane would feel obliged to support.

"Would you be willing to have your desk placed at the back of the lecture hall, so that whenever the students sit down for their lessons, they won't see you so very well? If they do not see you very often, then it won't distract them from listening to the professors. My apologies, but sometimes beauty can be a curse."

He was not discarding me! He merely wanted to place me in a spot where I would be the least amount of a distraction. And if that were merely a smokescreen for the truth, which was that he did not wish for the students to view a female amanuensis too often, then I would set aside my pride. After all, no matter Mr. Hanley's motive, I obtained what I wanted.

"As long as I am placed at a location where I can hear the professor's voice clearly enough to transcribe his words, then it will suffice," I assented.

"Very good. As I understand it, you have just moved to Milton."

"Yes, sir."

"I can give you three more days to settle your affairs of moving in. But you start work next Monday. Welcome to our staff."

I smiled.

"Thank you, sir. I promise, due to past circumstances, I will strive to be a worthy scribe."

"Past circumstances?"

"There was a time that I was not the best notetaker. So, I've spent the last few years trying to make up for that."

"You are honest."

"I don't want you to feel as if you are hiring a liar."

His eyes suddenly turned gentler.

"Well said, Miss Bennet. Be sure to arrive on Monday. Ten o'clock is your first lesson. It will be in the main hall."

"Who is the professor that I shall be the notetaker for, during that class?"

"Professor Hunnicutt."

When I left Mr. Hanley's office, I noticed that I was all alone in the hall. Since there was no one to spy on me, I skipped down the hall, did a little jig and then I began to leave. As I did so, I came across Mr. Hunnicutt.

"Well?" he asked, with a raised eyebrow.

"Are you a professor, Mr. Hunnicutt?" I asked amusingly, despite already knowing the answer.

"Yes. I teach architecture."

"Then I am your notetaker."

He cheered for me, and I laughed.

"Are you always this kind?" I asked.

"Yes, I am. A byproduct of being born plain."

"Well, I request that you continue to be nice to me. I need all the allies that I can get."

"Welcome to Granger Hall."

"Thank you. Now the trick is to last."

"Oh, beauty very much can be a curse when a woman is seeking employment," Kitty said as I was doing my best to make us a nice dinner. In our kitchen, I was undertaking to fry chicken and boil potatoes. Despite my efforts, I was still not used to the oven and stove, so I was doing my best to adapt.

I had told her about my day, and when I had reached the part in the story where Mr. Hanley had objected to my appearance more than my gender, Kitty was not surprised by this. Rather, it was evident that she had some experience in the matter.

"When I first arrived in Milton," she said, unpinning her hair as she sat down in a chair, "getting work was difficult. The only quality that I had to my name was my demeanor. However, from working in taverns, to even being an assistant, many labelled me as too attractive for the post, and I was dismissed."

"They really view beauty as a distraction?"

"Not just a distraction, but a dangerous hindrance."

"What way do we impede the progress of their work?"

"Beauty draws admirers."

I stopped preparing the butter for the potatoes, and I was able to deduce what she meant.

"And admirers bring potential conflict or scenes. Having admirers brings...complications. And they aren't wrong. Beauty can bring out rash desire on men's parts and potential jealousy on women's parts."

"Yes," Kitty confirmed, unbuttoning the sleeves to her dress.

"Welcome to the world, where if you are plain, no one notices you, but if you are handsome, the wrong sort notices you."

"*Welcome* to the world of employment. Sometimes, I miss when Jane was regarded as the handsome one, and we were nothing compared to her."

"Yes. It was all so much simpler back then."

Kitty came up to me.

"You're frying the chicken?" she asked.

"I learned," I said.

She looked skeptical.

"Believe me," I assured her. "It will taste good."

When we sat down to eat, Kitty was wearing her nightdress, with her robe on top of it. Her hair was wet from it being washed as she sat down to eat.

"Elizabeth," she advised me, "believe me. You will learn that there is no delight like bathing before you eat. It feels better that way. We have to cling to our happy moments where we may."

She bit into my chicken, and she groaned.

"You don't like it?" I asked, biting into it.

"I love it!" She said, between bites. "It is delightful."

I smiled.

"Boiling is easy and accomplishes much," I said, "but sometimes, other cultures do have a better idea."

"I've never tasted anything like this."

"And soon, you will never want it any differently. My apologies when there will be days that I will have to bake the meat."

We continued to eat.

"Kitty?" I said, looking at her.

"Yes?"

"When you and Jane first moved out here, were you scared?"

"What sort of question is that? Of course, I was scared. I told you so."

"But you seem so natural."

"I'm natural because I have to be. Sometimes, I look into the fire, get lost in my thoughts and then wonder what it would have been like if mama and papa had never gotten into that carriage. We would still be the ladies of Longbourn, father would be there to protect us, and Mr. Collins would still be giving tedious sermons in Kent. Then I choose to believe it, only for a second. Then the second comes to an end, and I wake up to realize that we are here." Her eyes suddenly looked wistful. "And you wonder how you got here and what life has in store for you? You even wonder if this is a bitter old joke, but you know that it's not."

"It's reality," I said, "it's the cold light of reality."

"Yes."

"I'm sorry," I urged. "I am being a bore."

"It's fine, Lizzy. You haven't said anything that I haven't already thought of."

We continued to eat.

I boiled water to take my bath in our washbasin, washed my hair, got dressed and went to my bedroom. When I entered, the place was done up in the best possible way, but it felt so empty without Jane there.

Sitting down, I lit another candle at my desk, for maximum light, and I began to write to Charlotte Lucas.

> Seeing Kitty sitting there, eating my best attempt at a dinner, and having the faraway look in her eye—well, it made me forlorn. How often I secretly and publicly ridiculed her and Lydia for their rambunctious and flirtatious demeanors. And now, to see Kitty so desolate, so broken—even if it was but a moment—it made me feel the inevitable thing: regret.
>
> Perhaps, I had been too hard on her before. Perhaps I stomped on her youthful energy and did not try to understand her. Either way, I would give anything for her bloom to be returned to her. But try as we might, we cannot go back. I can change nothing.
>
> And as for you, dear Charlotte, once more, I am most beholden to you. I know that I have thanked you so often, already, for not marrying Mr. Collins, out of devotion to our friendship. More and more, I am being shown the despair that can come from having no prospects. Only now am I aware of your sacrifice.

Charlotte, I miss you terribly, and wonder how I shall fare in this strange land.

Your friend of a profession,

Elizabeth Bennet

I sealed the letter and had it sent the next day.

Chapter 11

The Invitation

I was left with three days to prepare myself for work. Since I would no longer have much time of leisure, I had to live as much as I could in those remaining days.

The next morning, desirous to have company, I left with Kitty and went to the hotel. When I arrived, a mulatto woman, of medium brown skin, rushed up to Kitty and grabbed her hand. Judging by her uniform, I could tell that she was also a chambermaid.

"Kitty, did you hear the news?" she asked.

"No, I didn't!" Kitty replied, excited. Then she remembered me, and she touched my hand. "Raspberry[1], this is my sister, Elizabeth Bennet. Elizabeth, this is Raspberry Pitcher."

"Nice to make your acquaintance, Miss Pitcher," I said.

"Nice to meet you as well," she responded. "It would do better if you were to call me Rasby. I respond to that more readily."

"Very well, you may call me Lizzy. Or Eliza. Or Beth. Or

---

1. Raspberry was a REAL VICTORIAN name. Also, to make the reader aware, if you ever encounter a character with a strange name in this series, it is because of an attempt to be accurate to some names from real Victorian history.

Elizabeth. Or Betsy. It is just now that I am hearing how many variations of my name there really are."

"Even Bettie," Raspberry added.

"Oh, another one?" I said, rolling my eyes. "Makes sense, I suppose. Especially when you might be from a family where there are seven Elizabeths in each generation. That has been known to happen."

"My mother put a stop to that in advance. Then again, she did also like raspberries."

"I never met someone who didn't. My introductions interrupted your news."

"Yes, now I want to know more than ever!" Kitty declared. "Rasby, come on. You know we have only a matter of time before Frances comes out and gets mad at us for 'clumping'." She turned to me to explain. "Frances is our chief supervisor. Clumping is his term for whenever we congregate in public."

"Our employers prefer us to go unseen," Raspberry informed me, "the more invisible we are, the better."

"Then let's come away," I advised. "I don't want you both getting into trouble just because I am here. I'm visiting my friends on the second floor. If you escort me, you can look as if you are assisting me in some way."

"You think on your feet," Raspberry noted, "good. I don't need them to have another reason to sack me."

"Another reason?" I asked. Raspberry responded by pointing to her skin, and I understood the implications. As we walked up the steps to the second floor, Raspberry finally figured that she could unveil her news. And it was about time since she was practically bursting with excitement.

"The regiment is coming to Milton!" she professed.

"What?" Kitty cried.

"Yes! A regiment of her majesty's militia is coming to Milton." Kitty grabbed Raspberry's hand and began to jump up and down giddily.

"Rasby, do you mean it?"

"Cross my heart! I have it upon very good authority that they will be here within a fortnight."

"Oh, that is so wonderful!" Kitty cried. "If we get fortunate, then Lydia might come! Can you find that out for me?"

"I can write to my brother," Raspberry offered, "but I fear that the response might be here right when they come. You can write to your sister if she will be in the party."

"Lydia is awful at writing to us," Kitty elaborated. "If she does come to Milton, then we won't know of it until the day before."

"And how do you know this?" I inquired, desiring to know. "You mentioned your brother."

"Yes. His name is Plato. He's my younger brother. He was able to find a way to secure employment in the military, and he's one of the soldiers that will be settling here for the winter."

"He must be pretty awe-inspiring to have overcome such obstacles," I said, without shame or self-consciousness.

"Oh, he is," Raspberry said. "Plato has always been popular, and he is the sort that has the ability to make anyone like him. He was able to make enough friends who helped him obtain his post. When you see him, you will understand. He's different than me."

"In what way?"

"I can't explain it. He just has an aura. A nature that makes everyone see him for how he wants you to see him."

"Your brother is charming?" I asked.

"Yes."

"Which," Kitty encouraged, "in our times, is very refreshing."

"Even his Colonel likes him. Then again, from what Plato writes, Colonel Fitzwilliam does seem to be a different sort of man."

My eyes widened.

"Did you say Colonel Fitzwilliam?" I asked, my eyes widening.

"Ah, you know the Colonel, I gather?" she deduced.

"Yes, I do."

"Lizzy," Kitty realized, "isn't that the name of Mr. Darcy's cousin?"

Colonel Fitzwilliam was coming to Milton?

This week was continuing to bring so many surprises, and in the most unlikely of places.

"Yes," I confirmed. "Colonel Fitzwilliam is Mr. Darcy's cousin."

"Who's Mr. Darcy?" Raspberry asked.

"I'll tell you all about it when we have to clean out Mr. and Mrs. Hopkins's room," Kitty said. "Eliza, here's where we have to work. For look."

Up ahead, we saw a very sour man, wearing the proper attire of a hotel steward. He was of medium height, was slightly balding, and he had a natural dour look. Have you ever met someone who was sour in person, and their face constantly displayed it? That was how this man looked.

"Kitty and Rasby!" he hissed. "Stop being lax in your duties and get to work."

"Yes, Mr. Frances," Kitty and Raspberry said in unison, with an intimidated look on their faces. I hated Frances on sight! My disgust toward him was cemented when he looked cruelly on Raspberry.

"And you, girl, are always a meter away from being sacked. I look for a reason to go the full distance of dismissing you."

I was at my wit's end. Standing in front of them both, I faced down Frances.

"Sir, both women were assisting me on learning of the delights of Milton. Why are chambermaids not allowed to assist guests?"

Mr. Frances, clearly not used to being spoken to like such, flinched.

"By assisting me, are they not holding to their service?" I furthered. My question was rhetorical, and I didn't wait for him to respond. "Sir, you will excuse us."

He stuttered.

"Very well," he responded. "Begging your pardon, miss."

"I was not the one who was being offended."

Not wishing to remain, he bowed and left the hallway.

I turned to Kitty and Raspberry, with raised eyebrows.

"How did you do that?" Raspberry asked, amazed.

"I had one main trick up my sleeve."

"And what is that?"

"I'm not the one who works for him," I answered.

"I knew that I would like you! Now, come, Kitty," Raspberry said, grabbing her hand. "His patience will be at its furthest limits, and he will grow red in the face."

"But Rasby," I called after them, eager to know, "if Plato has made friends, can you write to him to ask if there is a man named Wickham in his regiment?"

"Wickham?" Raspberry asked, her face scrunched up from uncertainty.

"Never fear, Lizzy," Kitty said, "I'll tell her all about him."

They disappeared down the corner.

"Elizabeth," Margaret Hale said as I met her, Mrs. Hale, and Dixon in the parlor of their hotel room. "We now have a home."

"Do you?" I asked.

"Yes. It is the house in Crampton."

"The one that Mr. Darcy escorted us to?"

"Yes, that one."

"I thought that..."

I had recalled that she didn't want to move there, due to the bad experience that we shared. Reading my expression, Margaret thought it best to explain.

"It really is the ONLY option that is left to us," she elaborated, resigned. "And I was able to organize the setup of the house in a way where there would be room for all of us."

"Mr. Hale is there now, signing the rent," Mrs. Hale informed us.

"It will be nothing like Helstone," Dixon grunted, "we're to live amongst smoke."

"Dixon, you have the strength to endure it all," I stated.

"It is not myself that I am worried over, mark you all," Dixon declared. "This is not the place for ladies. And I don't care what this new house is to look like."

"I've heard horrors about the wallpaper," Mrs. Hale said, "but Mr. Hale seems to like the man who oversees that house: Mr. Thornton. I suspect that is the reason that the house is being chosen. They have become friends within the two days of knowing each other. I don't see how your father can prefer the company of these Milton men, Margaret. I do not understand it at all."

Margaret and I gave each other a look.

"Mr. Thornton?" I asked. "The Mr. Thornton that we met before?"

"Yes," Margaret answered.

"Your father likes him?"

"Yes."

And that would, undoubtedly, be the strangest news that I had heard all day.

"Fascinating," was the only response that I could administer to the situation.

"Yes," Margaret confirmed, "a very good euphemism for it."

When Mr. Hale returned, he was all in rapture.

"I have just dined with Mr. Thornton," he cried. "What an agreeable fellow. What's more, he has requested my services as being a pupil of mine."

"Has he?" Margaret asked, and once more, we exchanged a look.

"Yes, he has." Sitting down next to his wife, he placed Mrs. Hale's hand in his. "Dearest, this is wonderful news. With him signing on to private lessons, perhaps more of these manufacturers will follow."

"What inspires him to take lessons, I wonder?" Margaret asked, apprehensive. "After all, he is a manufacturer of a determined and set age."

"I have a theory on that score," Mr. Hale deduced, "and that is the desire for enlightenment. After all, who doesn't desire to better themselves? Such an inclination for self-enhancement is not confined to one region of England, Britain, or the world, for that matter. From Britain to Australia, from Australia to America, from America to Asia, and from Asia to Africa, one always prefers to be respected amongst one's peers. Milton ought to not be an exception. These manufacturers naturally wish to speak, converse and be respected amongst the most learned men from Oxford, Cambridge, and the like. Education and intellect are as much a currency as money, sometimes. Mr. Thornton wishes to better himself. I appreciate such an inclination, and I expect that he will be a valuable acquaintance. If only for conversation at least."

I looked at Margaret again, wondering how she was taking such news.

At last, when we were given a moment to converse with ourselves, Margaret was able to unleash her feelings.

"Of all the men for my father to befriend when taking two steps into a new town, it had to be Mr. Thornton's sort," she uttered.

"Did you tell your father about our first meeting him?" I asked. "He doesn't speak like a man who knows the truth."

"No, I haven't, because it is neither here nor there," Margaret advised, "I don't know why but I don't think it would be kind to tell father about Mr. Thornton's bad first impression. I think...Papa is lonely right now."

I scratched my chin, surprised by this honest confession.

"I must not make him desperate by trying to sour him against the first friend that he has made," Margaret furthered, "believe me, that is never kind to teach someone prejudice, even if I feel it myself. No, let my father like him, and I will have to be content with knowing the truth."

Her speech humbled me, for it rendered me a little disconcerted. It reminded me of another experience from my past. And a past acquaintance, by the name of Mr. Wickham, was involved.

"Very well," I said. "But Margaret, I will have to advise you."

"About what?"

"About the fact that, since Mr. Thornton may become friends with your father, that you will eventually have to encounter him."

"I hope that they will not be long and frequent interactions. I do not expect myself to have anything to say to him. Oh, I see him now, with that violent look in his eye and that hellfire of a temper. My father is free to like him, and he ought to. But I may safely promise you that I will never prefer the company of Mr. Thornton."

Since I had remained with the Hales the entire day, I was able to return home with Kitty.

"Rasby didn't know of a Mr. Wickham," Kitty informed me as we rode the omnibus home. "Plato has never mentioned him in her letters at all."

"Well," I gathered, "regiments can be large in number.

Perhaps Plato and Mr. Wickham don't move in the same sphere of acquaintance."

"I do not think so, Elizabeth," Kitty gathered. "Plato has always been very good at knowing names of everyone who serves around him. And Mr. Wickham is a popular man. Rasby will write to Plato about Mr. Wickham, but if she has not heard of him at this point, then it's unlikely that Mr. Wickham will be in the regiment. And I am curious. Colonel Fitzwilliam—you met him?"

"Yes, I did. When I was in London, he was at a few dinner parties that I attended with Mrs. Shaw, Edith and Captain Lennox."

"What manner of man is he?" Kitty asked.

"He is not very handsome, but after a while, you will not care. He is very charming, and he prefers women's company. And, since he is in a redcoat, you will admire him a great deal."

"Tease me all that you like, Lizzy, but there is nothing so very terrible about finding officers agreeable."

"You still prefer them to anyone else?"

"Yes, because heaven forbid that we spend our lives having any sort of fun."

"I just don't want you to be ridiculed by others."

Kitty looked at me shrewdly.

"More than how we are already ridiculed ever since we fell further in rank and position? Lizzy, we are poor now. What have we to lose?"

"Valid point. Very well. But we have one more thing that is worth keeping."

"And what is that?"

"Our self-respect."

"I have that. I respect the right to enjoy my life. After all, I have only one life to live."

"That is a bit of philosophy that I do not deny has some logic, but still, Kitty, please do not compromise yourself very much. I don't want others to cast aspersions at you."

"We are below anyone's notice now. I find freedom in that. Freedom, after all, is a poor woman's first and last resort."

I pinched her.

"What was that for?"

"For saying something witty. Even I don't deny that you said it well."

Kitty chuckled.

When we returned home and we stepped into our small lodgings, we were surprised to discover that there were two letters for us.

"The first is from Lydia!" Kitty cried, ripping open the letter. "It is about time. I haven't heard from her in weeks."

"Same with myself," I said removing my bonnet and coat. "What was it that she said when we asked her to write to us often? Oh yes, that's right! 'Married women do not often have time for writing'." I chuckled. "Mama would have agreed with her."

"She is coming to Milton!"

"Really?" I asked. "Then Denny is in Colonel Fitzwilliam's regiment now?"

"He must be."

"There must have been some sort of exchange being made."

"Whatever the reason, Denny is in Colonel Fitzwilliam's regiment, and he is coming to Milton, with the officers' wives in attendance. Lydia will hate Milton, I bet."

"She will find something to laugh at, I am sure," I noted, putting on my apron and going into the kitchen. "As long as she can find subjects of mirth, and men to pay attention to her, she will be happy. The smoke will not deter her."

"And soon it will not deter you. You still are disgusted by the hustle, smoke and bustle of Milton, Lizzy. I can see it in your eyes."

"Nothing is hidden," I said, beginning to make a salad. "I put it out there for all my acquaintances to see, if they ever wish to read the subtleties of my expressions."

"Very soon, you will grow accustomed to this place. Eventually, you will learn to like it."

"How long will that take?"

"For you? A couple years at least." She had joked, and I was aware of that.

"Who is the second letter from?" I asked, pulling the lettuce apart.

"Mr. Darcy!"

I stopped preparing our meal.

"What?"

"It's from Mr. Darcy."

Kitty looked at me and she could sense that I was uncomfortable.

"Eliza, I have to read it."

"Of course. Go on, I am not against hearing anything that he would have to say."

She opened the letter and read it.

Miss Bennet, Miss Elizabeth, and Miss Kitty,

I pray that I find you all in good spirits and good health. Miss Elizabeth, having encountered you two days ago has reminded me of the joys of meeting previous acquaintances while being in a strange town. Desirous to rediscover friends made from Hertfordshire, I would like to request the right to call on you all and pay my respects.

If you would be so kind as to accept, please write back to inform me of what day would be the best to arrange the visit.

Sincerely,

F. Darcy

When Kitty finished reading it, her cheeks were red. Looking in her eyes, she felt precisely as I did.

"Never mind, I was wrong," I uttered.

"Yes."

We looked around ourselves, at our small lodgings, and our obvious unsuccessful attempt to make it worthy of anyone above our station to wish to visit. Let alone the Master of Pemberley!

"If he were to take one step in here and see how we lived," I uttered. "I..."

"Yes," Kitty said, understanding what I felt. "But we also can't write back in the negative, because that would be rude."

"Yes, it would be. Therefore, there is only one thing to do. After all, you are right. We are poor now, and I see that there is freedom in one way. There is no point in hiding anything."

"What?" Kitty asked.

"I am going to tell Mr. Darcy the truth."

After we ate, I composed a letter. Kitty left briefly, to give our leftover food to a family who lived around the corner, by the name of Boucher.

Late that night, once more, I was sleeping alone in my bed, and I had the blankets wrapped around me tightly. The night was cold, and the room let some of the chill in.

I was convinced that I was right for sending the letter to Mr. Darcy. I was tired of there being secrets and misunderstandings between us.

Even more, I had time to reflect on my history with Mr. Darcy and Mr. Wickham. When Mr. Wickham had entered Meryton, and he very quickly made himself agreeable to everyone around him, including myself, I was beginning to see something.

I had been angry with Mr. Darcy ever since we first met and he slighted me, by refusing to dance with me and by thinking me to not be handsome enough to stand up with him. When Mr. Wickham came to Hertfordshire, having joined the regiment, Mr. Darcy's offenses against him naturally would endear me to Wickham. After all, when someone hates someone that you hate, you band together and find an ally. But when I heard Margaret declare that she would never tell her father about our first impression of Mr. Thornton, on the grounds that she did not want to affect their relationship, it left me wondering.

Mr. Darcy vs Mr. Wickham.

How quickly I had sided with the latter against the former. Yes, my anger for Mr. Darcy was initially sparked from our disastrous first encounter with each other, but that was MY experience. Mr. Wickham's telling me of how Mr. Darcy had robbed him of his inheritance and reduced him to a state of poverty, was *Wickham's* experience. It wasn't my prejudice to take up and share with him. Maybe Mr. Wickham was erroneous for trying to influence me into his way of thinking.

Then again...there was a more frightening aspect. After all, we are all adults who are responsible for our thoughts. Yes, others can be wrong for swaying us to their selfish cause. But, at the end of the day, it is mainly our fault for allowing ourselves to be swayed. Did I take a wrong step somewhere?

In the next second, I closed my eyes in vexation.

What was happening to me?

Mr. Wickham and I were very good friends! Why was I doubting him now?

Then I recalled Margaret's words. And yes, they did make sense!

What was Milton doing to me? It had the uncanny ability to make me confused.

Chapter 12

The Response

T he next afternoon, Elizabeth left her letter at the front office of the hotel and continued on her way. The letter was taken up to Mr. Darcy's room and left at his table while he was bathing.

When he finished, and Mr. Jefferson, his valet, was assisting him dress, he informed him of the letter.

"Who sent it?" Darcy asked.

"A Miss Elizabeth Bennet."

When hearing her name, Mr. Darcy froze, with his shirt's cuff still not fully buttoned.

"Sir?" Jefferson inquired.

"How long has it been since it arrived?" Darcy asked, his eye firmly on the letter.

"I was informed that it was hand-delivered at the front desk, and it only arrived but a quarter of an hour ago."

"Very good."

He allowed Jefferson to finish assisting him, but it felt like an eternity. When he finished, Darcy was on the verge of dismissing him when Jefferson spoke up.

"Unless I am mistaken," Jefferson theorized, "is this the same Elizabeth Bennet who walked three miles to Netherfield

Park to tend to her sister, Jane Bennet, when Miss Bennet was ill?"

"Yes, you are correct."

"And is this also the same Elizabeth Bennet whose parents passed away and she and her sisters were cast from their home by their cousin, Mr. Collins, who barely waited a month before he casually encouraged them to leave their home and threw them into the winds of other people's plans?"

Mr. Darcy was surprised by his valet's flare for the dramatic.

"Yes, Jefferson."

"And this would also be the Elizabeth Bennet who now has taken up residence in Frances Street with two of her sisters."

"Yes, Jefferson."

"And would this also be the Elizabeth Bennet who has taken employment at Granger Hall as a professional notetaker?"

"Yes."

Then Darcy realized that he just agreed to something that he was thoroughly ignorant of.

"What?"

"Am I incorrect?"

"I cannot deny or confirm that last bit of information because I am unaware of it. And how do you know of it?"

"Her sister, Miss Jane Bennet, is friends with Miss Fanny Thornton of Marlborough Mills. Well, Miss Thornton has a wonderful habit of telling her servants everything, without discretion."

"Ah," Mr. Darcy replied, knowingly, "Miss Thornton told her servants, you befriended her servants, and they told you."

"Sir, you are aware of my habit of viewing information like it is currency."

"Yes, and I appreciate your habits."

"Thank you, sir."

Sensing that Mr. Darcy wanted to read his letter in private, Jefferson began to leave.

"Jefferson?"

"Yes, Master Darcy," Jefferson said, turning back to him.

"How much information do you know?"

"Much," Jefferson said, with a twinkle in his eye. "Much."

He left Mr. Darcy alone.

"Servants," Darcy said to himself. "The Master shall always be the last to know."

At last, he turned around and looked down at the letter that Miss Elizabeth sent. His heart felt heavy at the sight of it.

There, on the front, was her name written, bold and true. The mere sight of it unnerved him.

What if it conveyed a negative response? What if she didn't wish for him to call on her? Nothing was so heavy than the unknown emotions of how a woman felt toward a man. Especially if the man was in love with the woman, but the woman was not in love with him.

He loved her!

After all this time, he still loved her.

While her anger toward himself had been long since done away, it appeared, he didn't know if her attitude toward him was merely polite or if it hinted at something more that could come.

Hope was a dangerous thing.

And now, when seeing the letter, he realized just how dangerous it had been. After all, when he had proposed to her, he had presumed that he understood her sentiments, and he had been proven to be mistaken.

This letter could show him how wrong he was now.

At last, he picked up the letter.

Then he set it down again.

He picked up the letter again, and then he stared at it.

From an intense sign of despair, Mr. Darcy placed the letter against his chest and pressed it against his heart.

Sitting down, he let the missive rest there.

How could he bear any negative response from her?

It would be a shocking blow. When she rejected him, he had felt as if every bit of his skin was being bombarded with invisible rocks. He had survived it before, but he was not so certain that his resolve could suffer another great blow.

For a fleeting moment, he wondered if he was foolish for sending her a message. She did not welcome his attentions before. But she had been perfectly content to see him yesterday.

Such are the emotional states of people when they are in love. The constant agony of their emotions can make the mundane into a marvel. The most trivial matter into a battlefield where war can be waged. Internally, of course.

At last, Darcy gathered his courage—for he had much of it— and he opened the letter. Preparing himself, he began to read.

> *Dear Mr. Darcy,*
>
> *We thank you very much for your desire to pay a visit to our humble home at Frances Street. It is always lovely to meet friends. Yet, it is in consideration to your sensibilities, on many accounts, that I fear we must decline it. Understand that this is NOT out of any desire to not further our acquaintance with you, but rather to shield you from encounters that might be uncomfortable for you.*
>
> *Mr. Darcy, to be frank, our home is not a domicile that you would wish to visit. Frances Street is...we have been reduced in the eyes of the world and while my sisters have succeeded at making our residence comfortable, quaint, and very livable, you might be apprehensive at the mere presence of it.*
>
> *As much as I do not wish to recall our last encounter, but I must. You made it quite plain that you did not take pleasure in attaching yourself to relations who are so decidedly below your own. Well now, we are even lower. I tell you this now, because I would fear the look that you would exude when seeing the street on which we live and the house in which we reside.*
>
> *I, myself, have felt shame over this degradation. It would be useless to deny that. However, I am getting used to it, and*

learning to feel the shame less keenly by every moment. Rather, I am doing all in my power to be proud of the fact that all my sisters have done well to not give into despair over our unfortunate circumstances, but rather, has done everything to recover and continue on. Such ability to adapt must recommend itself!

Yet, I wish to be candid with you. Also, you deserve no less, for disguise, of any sort, is your abhorrence. I would not ask you to visit, for I fear that you might not enjoy the experience.

However, I look forward to us continuing our acquaintance if you care to still do so after receiving this letter.

Thank you for your kind offer.

Yours etc.

Elizabeth Bennet

When closing the letter, Darcy was stricken with all sorts of emotions!

She had rejected the offer for a visit, but it was not out of a desire to not see him!

After all, he knew enough about her character to be aware that if she did not *truly* want to see him, she would have been frank about it.

No.

She did not want him to pay a visit because she thought she would be ashamed for him to enter their house and see how they lived.

And see all that they lost.

Shame: that very thing that had initially prevented him from proposing to her before. And, when thinking on the matter, she was correct. Frances Street really was an area of destitution and poverty. And that's where they lived. Then would she be ideal for him?

His heart said yes.

But his mind said no. Again!

If he did take a trip down to Frances Street, and he did see the circumstances that they lived in, perhaps this would glean some more knowledge on the matter.

But rather, he had a better idea.

"Frances Street?" Mr. Thornton echoed. "Why do you wish to know about that place?"

The next day, he had paid a visit to Mr. Thornton at Marlborough Mills, in hopes that Thornton would know a little bit about that area of Milton. Thornton had met him in his office but was needed to make his rounds and oversee everything. So, Darcy followed him through the halls, past all the workers. Not used to the sight of so much labor around him, and usually unaccustomed to the fluffs of cotton in the air, Darcy coughed a little.

"Just a mere bit curious," Darcy said, removing his handkerchief and holding it over his nose and mouth.

"It is amusing to see you walk through here." Thornton chuckled as they climbed the steps that helped Thornton oversee everyone in the factory, to make sure that no one was slacking on their responsibilities. Darcy climbed the steps with him and, he could not deny, there was something mesmerizing about seeing all these downtrodden workers, hard at work, with the white cottons moving through the air like larger snowflakes.

"Yes," Darcy acknowledged, "Indeed, I must look entirely out of my element."

"Nothing more or less than a man whose townhouse is from the South walking into a factory in the North," Thornton replied. "Very well, I can see that you don't want me to pry into your affairs."

"I don't wish to be elusive," Darcy explained. "There is just no story to tell yet. So, I don't wish to waste your time."

"Very well. Have you ever been to the *seedier* sides of London? The parts where no one in the aristocracy would dare to tread. Where gypsies and beggars dwell, and if you walk down it, they beg you for coins?"

"Yes. Well, in truth, I have never really walked down such streets, but rather, I have driven past them."

"And that is precisely the answer that I would have expected. Well, picture that in your mind. That is Frances Street. People on that street do their best to have an air of gentility, but they are...what they are. They do live in dire conditions, and they are always struggling to get by. Milton's color is already grim, but there, the grim rests hardest. Here in the North, a man such as myself would brave walking down such a street. But you...are you intending to take a trip there?"

Darcy scratched his lip.

"There is someone who resides there, who I have had a past acquaintance with."

Thornton crossed his arms over his chest, turning to Darcy, interested.

"Really? Mr. Darcy, of Pemberley, Derbyshire! To know someone who would live there."

"It is of small consequence," Darcy lied. "It is a family of ladies who lost their country estate, due to an entailment to the male line. When their parents passed away, their cousin claimed ownership of their home, and the sisters were forced to live elsewhere. Three of them have taken up residence in Frances Street."

"From living in the country to Frances Street? They must have fallen very far down indeed."

"So, it may seem."

"And you said these were a set of sisters?"

"Yes."

Thornton did not reply, but he gave Darcy a discerning look.

Darcy noticed this, but he decided to act as if he took no note of it.

"Are these the Bennet sisters that you and Fanny speak of, by any chance?" Thornton asked.

"It is them."

"Very well," Thornton replied, "actually, there is someone here who is more of an authority on that Street than myself. You can speak with him if you wish."

"I don't know."

"The choice is yours. He's by the spinner there, with the long curly hair." Darcy followed Thornton's eyes and saw the man, and the state of his clothes. "Then again, his clothes give a proper indication of what Frances Street is like." The man's clothes were gray, dirty, and gave all the indication of one who labored during the day and went home to a humble shack. "His name is Boucher. He might know about these ladies."

Seeing that there was no harm to it, Darcy wondered if maybe he should meet this man. After all, since the Bennet sisters had been living there for so long, perhaps he knew of them.

"Do you mind if I talked to Boucher in your office?"

"It would be no trouble. Would you like me to join you?"

"I think I could overpower him if he decided to get vicious," Darcy quipped.

"He won't. He's not an angry man. Just a weak one."

Darcy did not find this criticism to the man as being rude on Thornton's side...because Thornton would know better than anyone.

Mr. Darcy went to Thornton's office and waited. Soon, the door opened, and Thornton's overseer entered, followed by Boucher.

"Mr. Darcy, this is John Boucher. John Boucher, Mr. Darcy of Pemberley, in Derbyshire."

The overseer left them alone.

"Sir," Mr. Darcy said, bowing.

Seeing this illustrious man bowing to him flustered Boucher. Uncertain, and insecure around such a more illustrious man than himself, Boucher bowed clumsily.

Taking one look at Boucher, Darcy comprehended Thornton's assessment of Boucher's character. This unfortunate creature didn't seem like a very independent sort of fellow. He was not short, but nor was he tall. His figure was clearly a little malnourished, his face had a defeated look, and he had a flat nose. While these features were neither offensive to the eye, nor vicious in appearance, a want of happiness would have been needed to lighten his features. He had curly reddish-brown hair that fell behind his ears and his eyes had a blank look in them. Seeing this tall stern man looking down at him only added to Boucher's insecurities. His shoulders slackened under this wealthy man's gaze and fine clothing.

"Sir?" Boucher voiced, "I was told that yer asked 'bout me."

"Indeed, I did."

"What do yer need of me? I haven' done anything."

"No, I can assure you, that you were not asked here for any assumed wrongdoing. I merely wished to inquire about something that I think you may know about."

Boucher squinted.

"That *I* may know 'bout?"

"Yes, sir. As I understand it, you reside on Frances Street."

"Yea, I do, sir."

"What manner of street is it?"

"Well...it's a street."

Darcy leaned back. He could see that he was not going to get much out of this fellow.

"By any chance, do you know of a family of sisters who have taken up residency there? They came up from the South."

Boucher's eyes widened.

"Yer wouldn' be talkin' bout the Bennet sisters, would yer?"

"Indeed, I am. You know them?"

Boucher chuckled.

"We all know 'em. Anotha one jus' moved in but couple days ago. Many of the men say than' goodness."

"Why do they say thank goodness?"

"Because they fancy 'em, I reckon. Sometimes, the lads need a bonny face to look on, yer understand. And theirs is a picture."

Mr. Darcy's eyes narrowed even more, and this made Boucher cease chuckling.

"Are you well-acquainted with the Bennets?"

"Me? Naw. But me wife is. Sometimes they give her spare food for our little-uns."

"You have children?"

"Six, sir."

This boded well for Darcy. He feared that Boucher might have begun to take an interest in the Bennet sisters. Without even being aware of it, he found himself strangely protective over all three of them.

"Do you know if any men have taken an interest in the three ladies?"

"Well, I know, fo' a fact, that men have taken an interest in two of them, but the ladies don' take an interest back. It's not that they are prudish, nothin' like that. They jus' don't notice when men notice 'em back. They jus' take the men's compliments of 'em in good fun and keep 'bout their business. Me wife don' ever hear mention of any men come to visit 'em either. In fact, no one does. Strange, when I come to think 'bout it."

"Why?"

"Well, they clearly come fro' good family. That much is certain by how they dress and how me wife tell me 'bout how they act. She say that some of the things in their house clearly came from some estate they were raised on. They were from the South, yer see? And they must have been ladies of some sort. So, why no one visits them from where they come from is strange, I reckon."

"So, you would say that they 'stick out' from the usual Frances Street inhabitants?"

"Oh, ver' much! It's obvious that they have none to look aft' them, cause' if they did, then they wouldn't have to sink so low. Then again, none of us deserve to be there." Here his eyes turned misty from sadness. "My wife and little-uns def'ly don' deserve it. No child should have to live like that, yer' understand."

"Yes," Darcy replied, surprised by the sudden tinge of sympathy that he felt for the man.

On the other side, Boucher suddenly felt a tinge of disinterested protectiveness that was unlike him. A sense of chivalric duty that was selfless.

"Beggin' yer' pardon, sir," he uttered, "but yer' askin' these questions cause of innocent curiosity, right? There's no harm yer' thinkin' bout? Cause those girls is innocent. They haven' done anythin' to deserve—"

"I can assure you, sir," Darcy voiced, stonelike, "I have no pretensions of the kind. I merely ask it out of...concern for their welfare."

"Oh, well then, tha's good. Sir, please forgive me for soundin' like that. I was just...concerned too."

Darcy relaxed.

"Yes. Forgive my sharp tone."

Realizing that the poor man must have felt so intimidated, and that he had been beneficial in educating Darcy on the Bennet sisters' situation, Darcy felt that Boucher should not walk away empty-handed.

Reaching into his purse, Darcy pulled out four pounds.

When seeing it, Boucher's eyes lit up.

"For your children, sir," Darcy said, for the sake of encouraging the man to spend it on food and not drink. "And for your wife."

"Yeah, thank yer', sir," Boucher said. "The missus will be so glad!"

Giggling, Boucher left.

Afterwards, Thornton entered the office, for it was time for his workers to have their reprieve. They all exited the factory, and like one large gray mass, they exited the Mill and went to the nearest pub or place of rest.

Darcy had been standing by the window that overlooked the mill's grounds, so he was able to see their exodus. Watching them eagerly leave was amusing to him, and Thornton noticed this.

"From this angle, humanity is always agreeable to watch," Darcy said.

"Yes, it is. Then you have to be forced to get closer to them, and then everything changes. Did Boucher tell you anything useful?"

"Yes, he did. Thank you for the suggestion." Suddenly, Darcy's eyes wandered back to the view because something distracted him. A fleck of purple amongst the gray masses. "Miss Hale?"

"What?" Thornton asked, turning to where he looked. There, accidentally being jostled along with the crowd—having to make her way through them—was Margaret Hale.

She was wearing a blue dress and bonnet, with a flattering purple coat over it and black gloves. Not meaning to be overcome by the crowd, Margaret Hale backed up against a wall, holding her purse close to herself.

Both men looked at each other, quizzical.

"This is a conversation for a later date, isn't it?"

"Possibly so."

When both men turned back to the crowd, the fleck of purple that was Miss Margaret Hale, was gone.

Chapter 13

A Kind Gesture

"Elizabeth!" Margaret cried.

"Margaret!" I cried back.

With it being my last day before I had to begin working, Margaret and I had taken it as my last chance to walk around that area of Milton, to get a better idea of my surroundings. She and I had taken a brief separation because I wanted to enter a butcher's shop to see how the meat was there. Now that I had taken up a definite situation, I needed to know where the best places to shop were.

Having taken an interest in the mills that were up ahead— one of those mills belonged to the man who had been so very rude to us—Margaret told me that she would meet me outside the shop on the corner.

Very quickly, I left the butcher's shop. The meat there was abominable. When I did so, I saw that the streets suddenly had become filled with workers who were coming down the street in droves.

"When did this happen?" I gasped, a little overwhelmed by the throng who were about to come my way.

"You clearly are new here, I reckon," a flower-girl said to me, with her basket full of posies. "At this time of day, the factory people pour out of there, like streams. Be careful to be firm because they can accidentally end up pulling you along with them. Try and stay back against the walls of the shops, or you'll fall into their path."

I followed her instruction, until I saw a fleck of purple moving amongst the crowd, against her will.

"Margaret!" I had cried.

"Elizabeth!" she wailed.

Without thinking, I left my safe place and moved through the crowd. It was, quite possibly, one of the grandest physical struggles I had ever endured. Literally, with every step I took, I was being pushed back again. The progress and speed to which these factory workers moved was intensified by their desire to escape the mills. It could be rendered as only natural. After all, I had seen the inside of Marlborough Mills. If I worked there every day, I would probably eagerly await my great escape.

The crowd consisted of men and women. They came rushing along, with bold fearless faces, and loud laughs and jests, particularly aimed at all those who appeared to be above them in rank or station. The tones of their unrestrained voices, and their carelessness of all common rules of street politeness, unnerved me greatly. The women, without fear, were loud, and the men were impertinent.

As I tried to move upstream and Margaret attempted to move downstream, we both were the mirrors of each other, experiencing the same thing. Men looked on us in temptation, commenting on our faces, and the women made comments about us. Some even went so far as to touch our clothing as we tried to pass them. Their faces pressed into my vision with sharp clarification. With no fear, their eyes analyzed my person.

Eventually, Margaret and I met each other and grabbed hands.

"Let's remove ourselves from this!" Margaret cried.

"Come then!"

Incidentally, someone knocked into us, and we fell out of

the throng's path, and into a narrower part of the street. We had no time to breathe.

Just as we were knocked out of the crowd, we fell into the way of a carriage that had just begun to take off and ride down the street.

Despite our best efforts, Margaret and I were so shocked and alarmed that we felt it hard to move.

The rider pulled the horses' reins, in an attempt to slow the horses down. However, it was too late. The horses were about to collide into us.

Suddenly, we felt two hands wrap themselves around our waists and pulled us out of the carriage's way.

The horses had slid right to a halt a little past where Margaret and I stood.

We turned to the hands that had yanked us out of the way. We both looked up into the face of a large man. He had dark brown hair, almost black. His face was round, he wore a brimmed cap, had the same dark gray trousers, shirt, waistcoat, and jacket that the other workers had. His face was clean, however, and he had strong and compassionate eyes.

"My apologies for grabbin' yer like that," he uttered. "But it was the only way."

"Of course," I rushed out, "you saved us."

"Yes," Margaret added, "indelicacy doesn't matter in this case. We are much obliged to you, sir."

We were interrupted by the rider of the carriage. Having stopped his horses, he looked down on us, concerned.

"Are you alright!" he cried, desperately. "My apologies, missuses! I didn't mean for that to have happened."

"We understand," I assured him. "We were pushed into your path and there was nothing that could be done."

Next to me, Margaret opened her purse and was about to pay the man who had saved our lives.

"No charge," the man said, "I was just doin' my proper service."

"But you saved us, Mr..."

"Higgins," he uttered, "Nicholas Higgins."

He tipped his hat to us, and he looked at the rider.

"Hullo, Riker," Mr. Higgins said to the driver.

"Higgins."

Both men knew each other.

"Whereabouts are you headed?" Higgins asked the man.

"High Street."

Nicholas Higgins turned to us.

"Are you headed for that area?" he asked.

"Yes," Margaret said. "I'm staying at the hotel."

"I can drop you off there," the driver, Riker, said.

"Oh, you don't need to do that," I answered, politely.

"It would be a pleasure, and it will make up for what almost happened."

"Ah, let him give yer a good turn," Higgins said. "Sometimes, a man needs to make up for somethin' that could have gone very wrong."

"Very well," I said, "if we are not being an imposition."

"I'd be much obliged," Riker said. We turned to Higgins, a little apprehensive.

"Don' worry," Higgins said, "yer can trust him. There's no trick here."

"Very well," Margaret said, "we are most obliged to you both."

Nicholas Higgins offered us his hand and helped us into the carriage. When we got in, we were surprised to see a little girl that was already in there.

"Hullo," she said. "Are either of you my new governess?"

Margaret and I looked at each other. This man was conveying a little girl somewhere, by herself.

"No, I am afraid not," I said.

Mr. Higgins closed the door behind us, and Riker drove on. As he did so, we looked out of the window, and we saw that Mr. Nicholas Higgins was watching the carriage drive down the lane.

"Perhaps we may never see him again," I said.

"Yes, it is not likely," Margaret said, beside me.

As we drove along, all apprehensions faded. Seeing this little girl in the carriage, we knew that we were in safe hands.

"I am Miss Elizabeth Bennet," I began.

"And I am Miss Margaret Hale," Margaret added. "We apologize for intruding upon your ride. Mr. Riker was very kind and offered to give us a ride to High Street."

"Can you forgive us for intruding upon your company?" I asked, smiling down at her, with my eyes alight.

"I am not upset," the little girl said, "I was lonely anyway."

Margaret and I were startled by her honest confession. That was the one true thing about children; they were unafraid to speak as they felt.

"Well," Margaret said, "I hope we may be of service."

"What is your name?" I asked.

"Molly. Molly Gibson."

"Well, Miss Molly, your dress is very pretty," I commented.

"Thank you," she said. "Why aren't you my governess?"

"Well," Margaret replied, "I have not the amount of education that allows me to be a governess."

"And neither do I."

"You both seem nice."

"We hope to be," I replied, "thank you. You seem like a lovely girl yourself."

"Thank you. My last governess wasn't so nice at all. She was mean and it made her look ugly."

Margaret and I smiled.

"Well," Margaret replied, "hopefully your next governess will not be so rigid and cruel."

"I don't think so," Molly replied. "Every type of governess I've seen since coming to England has been mean. I miss home."

"Where was home before now?"

"Australia."

"Really?" I marveled. "I've always wanted to go to Australia."

"It's the best place ever," Molly cried. "I miss it ever so much. Even though the spiders are very big."

"Did your parents have to move here?"

"My parents died."

"Oh, I am so sorry!" Margaret gasped.

"I know how you feel," I added, "I lost my parents as well."

"My mother died when I was very little," the girl responded, "when I was three, and now I am six. But my father died because he was sick. He looked after me a lot and we always were close to each other. It's not fair. And he was a doctor. Why did he have to get sick?"

"Oh, I am so very sorry," Margaret said. "Do you have any more family? Is that why you came to England?"

"Yes, miss. I have come to live with my uncle. My Uncle Virge. He is my mother's brother."

"And is he kind to you?"

"He tries. He tries very hard. But he's nothing like my father. No one was like my father."

"He must have been a great man," I observed.

"Oh, yes, miss. He was the greatest father ever. It's not fair. It's not."

"No, it's not."

Eventually, we reached High Street, the carriage stopped, and we prepared for Mr. Riker to open the door for us. Before that, we heard raised voices. It was clearly Mr. Riker trying to tell someone of how he had escorted two new women here, with Molly Gibson still inside.

The carriage door was yanked open.

"I don't care who they are," the voice boomed, "you do not put strangers in a carriage with Molly!"

The man's face came into view, and it was time for me to be in for another shock.

"Miss Bennet?"

"Mr. Hanley!"

There, before me, was Mr. Hanley, my employer.

"Well," I gasped, "this is a wretched second impression."

"Yes," Mr. Hanley said, his voice faltering when realizing that I was the stranger. "Yes, it is."

Seeing as how he was not going to offer his arm, I placed my hand in front of him, and he took the message. Taking my hand, he helped me down from the carriage, then he did so with Margaret. Last, he grabbed Molly by the waist, picked her up and carried her from out of the carriage.

He crouched down and looked Molly in the eye.

"Sorry that I was not there to fetch you," Mr. Hanley apologized, "but I hear that you were well-treated."

"I was, Uncle. These ladies were my companions."

Mr. Hanley looked up at me.

"So," I gathered, "Virge is short for Virgil?"

"She calls me that," he said, referring to Molly. Next, he turned to Margaret.

"Mr. Hanley, this is my friend, Miss Hale."

"Nice to make your acquaintance, Miss Hale."

"Thank you," Margaret responded. "You have a lovely niece."

"My last bit of family left."

I bit my lip, slightly aghast that Mr. Hanley said such an open thing. When I first met him, he immediately struck me as the sort of man who was closed off.

I bent down and took Molly's hand.

"It was nice to have met you, Miss Gibson." I turned to Hanley. "Please do not be upset with Mr. Riker. He was just doing us a service, in repentance for almost running us over. That was not his fault either. Sometimes, life just chooses to knock everyone over at the same time."

Mr. Hanley looked at me, inquisitive.

"You are a unique sort, Miss Bennet."

"I know."

I patted Molly's cheek. Margaret and I went into the hotel.

On our way to Mrs. Hale's room, we passed Kitty and Raspberry.

"How goes the day?" Margaret asked them.

"It's work," Kitty responded, "that's all that can be said of that."

"And what about you both?" Raspberry asked. "Your faces have an interesting look to them."

"Because this day has knocked us about a little too much," I commented.

"Welcome to our lives."

Chapter 14

The First Day

S ince the only mirror in our house was small, I was not able to get a good view of my image. I had worn my most professional dress, which was also my most flattering, and I stood in front of Kitty.

"How do I look?" I asked. "Is there anything out of place?"

"One bit of white thread that's on your sleeve. Hold on."

She took the thread off and then looked at me once more.

"That's the only problem with darker-colored gowns," she noted, "it's easy to see when lint falls upon it. Either way, for the moment, you look perfect."

She did the same thing to me. I confirmed that she looked proper, and we left home together. Our stops on the omnibus were at different points and soon I was standing in front of Granger Hall.

"Well, Elizabeth," I said to myself, "brace yourself. After all, it's only the rest of your life."

Fortifying any negative reaction to my first day of work, I went into Granger Hall and reported to Mr. Hunnicutt.

"Ah, Miss Bennet," Mr. Hunnicutt said, jovially. "First day on the job. Are you nervous?"

"Quite so," I smiled, happy that I always began the day with

155

Mr. Hunnicutt. He was a lighthearted man and that was the sort of company that I enjoyed. He also had the good fortune to not be handsome at all. That left him obliged to be agreeable to the rest of the world, because his personality had to be his chief asset. "I do not deny it."

"Well, you will begin the day in an easy fashion," he said, handing me a portable desk that contained paper, pen, and ink within it. "You will be my notetaker for the morning. I teach a variety of subjects. It's German today. Don't worry, I speak at a nice slow pace—but not a monotone one."

"Oh, that is very good," I said, following him to the lecture hall with my desk in my arms, "I had one governess who never learned that speaking in the same droll tone rendered her lessons unlearnable."

"Yes, I had many professors who suffered under that presumptuous habit that showing any interest in subject matter when lecturing meant one was unprofessional," Mr. Hunnicutt added, laughing. "Blast them all. My experience at university was not a good one. I had resolved it within myself to become an educator, to spare students from the experience that I once had to endure."

"It is always good to end the vicious cycle."

We entered the hall, and I began to set up my desk in the back corner of the room.

Soon after I had my paper, pen and ink placed on the desk, students began to arrive. As the men entered, a few of them glanced my way, then they looked back again.

I smiled gently at them, for the sake of being friendly, but I displayed no other signs of warmth—but that had proven to be too much. The students composed of men who were of the middle class, who could not afford private tutors. Some of them were in their twenties and thirties.

When a couple of them saw me, they stopped in their tracks, changed directions, and came over to the nearest chairs to myself. Their close proximity to me made me very uneasy. It wasn't because I immediately took a disdain for men who might find a woman's company agreeable, but that they would try and engage me in discussion. My vocation was to be silent and write down every major point that Mr. Hunnicutt would think were the key aspects of the lessons.

Fortunately, I was not left to fend for myself. When seeing the men who were placing themselves near me, with every intent to pay me notice, Mr. Hunnicutt informed them to come closer to the front. The students obeyed and I gave Mr. Hunnicutt a look of gratitude. He noticed, smiled gently, and began his class.

Despite having never taken German in the whole of my life, this was a very easy class to take notes for! Mr. Hunnicutt was exquisite at enunciation, he wrote down the information on the blackboard in clear letters, and he did speak at his promised pace. I was able to get down all the notes of chief import, and even did side bullet points. Sometimes, I didn't even need to use shorthand.

"You are very good," I complimented him when the class came to an end. Holding my desk under my arm, I escorted him out of the room.

"Why thank you, dear lady," he responded, taking my desk from out of my arms to carry it for me. "And, as you know, I must peruse your notes before you copy them."

"I understand. How long have you known German? For you speak it as if it is your second language."

"That's because it's my first. I'm a German native."

I blinked, surprised.

"You are?"

"Yes," he chuckled, "I understand your confusion on the matter. My mother was German, and my father was English. I was born in Germany, but when I was nine years old, my mother passed away, father brought me to England, and I had to learn to adapt to a whole other world—a world that would remind me that I was a foreigner. When I went to Cambridge, I had mastered the English accent, so I could start over. After all, my father's name was Hunnicutt, and I sounded like everyone else. I was the best in German classes, and when I graduated, I thought it wise to put my native tongue to the test. I taught German, and it's been working splendidly for me ever since."

"We all seem to come from somewhere else, don't we?" I asked him as we entered his office, and I handed him my notes.

"Yes, we do. But the world is content to only make us all feel like outsiders. Now, let us see."

I handed him my notes and he began to read.

"Oh, your notes are in two columns?" He observed.

"It's a habit of mine."

"I like it."

He put on his spectacles and began to read it, while pacing back and forth.

At last, he finished reading it, lowered the notes and looked at me over the brim of his spectacles. Here came the moment of truth.

"Very good," he replied. "This is proper notetaking!"

I sighed, relieved.

"For a moment, I thought you were about to say something awful."

"Well, I wasn't. This is how I wish for you to always take notes."

"How many copies should I make?" I asked.

"Two. Afterwards, you may enjoy your lunch. When you finish, I will introduce you to Professor Dennison. He teaches Italian."

"By any chance, does he have any Italian in him?"

"I never asked, but I know that it is Mr. Hanley that does."

My eyes widened.

"Mr. Hanley is part Italian?"

"Yes, you would not think of it when you look at him, poor fellow. He has not the charisma, romantic inclinations, and spark of life that marks the Italian man. Then again, traits are not wholly specific to any nationality. Now, if you don't mind, you must indulge me on something. I like music."

"So do I," I said as I sat in the corner of his office, placed my desk on the table and began to prepare making copies. "I am not talented in the line of music, but I admire it."

"Well, then hopefully, you will not begrudge me on my guilty pleasure. When I am not teaching, I love to listen to music."

In the other side of his office, he opened a chest and there was a phonograph.

"You have a phonograph!" I gasped.

"I do! Edison was a genius when he invented this contraption."

"But his ideas would be nothing without the discoveries of Édouard-Léon Scott de Martinville."

"You know about Scott?" Mr. Hunnicutt remarked, impressed.

"Oh yes! The clever fellow. Edison improved on the original model, and now here we are! Wasn't one of the first songs to be recorded on it 'Au Claire de la Lune'?"

"Yes. And that is precisely what we are about to listen to."

I sat there, excited, as the music began to play. What an ingenious thing!

Like a cascade of perfect melodies, 'Au Claire de la Lune' began to quietly play from the machine and I was enraptured.

"Music," Mr. Hunnicutt sighed, sitting down, and beginning to go over reading some papers, "the pleasures of society."

"Yes," I remarked, "be those pleasures from polished or unpolished societies. Any culture can understand music. It is the language of life."

Together, we sat there, with him looking over his work and

me copying notes. We didn't speak again the entire time, and I was at peace.

If every day could be like this, then I do believe I could adapt to a life of profession with grace.

After I ate my lunch, Mr. Dennison was punctual in addressing me.

And it was very quick to deduce that he and I would both hate each other. Quite a different person than Mr. Hunnicutt, Mr. Dennison was cold, severe, and didn't have the handsome features to apologize for his disposition. He was grotesque from without and from within. Even Mr. Hunnicutt evidently didn't like him.

"Why didn't you warn me that he was the worst man in the world?" I whispered to Mr. Hunnicutt as I prepared my desk.

"Because I have never seen him around ladies. I thought he would be better around you lot. My mistake. He hates life, and that's all there is to it."

Fortunately, I didn't have to speak to Mr. Dennison, but only take notes.

And he did show the irony of life: he was a phenomenal instructor. He spoke loud, well, clear and there was passion in his voice. It was evident that he had a love for the Italian language and for the Italian people.

It was even more ironic, because if he ever actually did meet an Italian, I wonder if they would even like him? Either way, his love for Italian culture rested in its proper place and he was another professor who was easy to serve as a notetaker.

When I finished, I had to submit to his higher opinion, and he had to critique my writing style.

Yes!

I had to sit there and watch this disagreeable man look over every word that I had written.

"This is intolerable," he uttered, "I don't like columns in notes. And bullet points."

"I thought it would be easier for your students to make sense of everything if it was laid out in such a fashion."

"You suppose wrongly. Your handwriting is also too feminine."

"I never met a man who cared for that."

"And your presence in my classroom is most distracting. Too much is in my favor when I argued that there should not be a female notetaker. And I was right."

"That is quite enough, sir!" came a voice to my right. Turning to who came to my defense, my jaw dropped at his sudden and most unexpected arrival.

"Mr. Darcy!" I uttered, my voice low.

Mr. Darcy was standing in the doorway of the lecture hall.

Chapter 15

Mr. Darcy to the Rescue

M r. Darcy had everything to recommend him!
From his sharp eyes, his fierce gaze, his tall and
imposing person, he left Mr. Dennison in awe. Also,
since his clothing and stance displayed the status of his position
in society, when Mr. Darcy stepped forward, I saw Mr. Dennison's eyes widen and guessed he felt the power of the man.

"Your tone is most egregious," Mr. Darcy declared. "Most
unprofessional. What sort of talk is this that you bestow it upon
a lady?"

"Are you a student?" Mr. Dennison sputtered.

"Do I look like a student?"

"Are you one of our patrons?"

"Do I look foolish enough to finance you, sir?" Mr. Darcy
questioned, very imposing. Unable to even notice what I was
doing, I smiled happily upon him. "Now, I ask you, what right
have you to speak to her in such a cold manner?"

"Well...she is my subordinate."

"Your subordinate?" Mr. Darcy echoed, incensed. "You use
that as justification for such outright and shameful prejudice?
This will not inherit and is unbecoming from a 'supposed' superior man."

"I am a professor here!"

"And a professor always has a superior to answer to. Or at the very least, colleagues to answer to. Let us make your case to them."

"I do not answer to you."

I am surprised how we humans can allow ourselves to be degraded, but when another of us are, we feel our courage rise and we rally to their defense. Now that Mr. Dennison was being unkind to Mr. Darcy, I was not in the mood to suffer fools to pass.

"Mr. Dennison," I hissed, "Mr. Darcy is a distinguished and highly respected man in the ton, as well as an Oxford Donne. Also, he comes to my defense out of compassion and consideration. I will thank you not to criticize or cast aspersions on his character for coming to my defense. Attack me as you wish, for I can assure you that it shall fall on indifferent ears that rises to the occasion of not being intimidated by you or any other. Is that understood?"

Mr. Dennison dropped my papers on the chair next to him.

"This all is highly unorthodox."

"Take us to your colleagues, and we shall see to what degree it is," Mr. Darcy furthered.

———

Mr. Hunnicutt looked over the notes that I had taken, while Mr. Dennison and I stood in front of his desk, with Mr. Darcy standing behind me.

Every now and again, I turned in his direction and gave him a look. He replied with one in kind.

At last, Hunnicutt lowered the papers and rubbed his eyes.

"What complaint do you have for the content of these notes, Dennison?" Hunnicutt asked, weary.

"I protest to the format," Mr. Dennison responded, "the

second that I see columns in my notes will be the day that pigs fly."

"Then there will be pork soaring through the clouds by morning," I retaliated. "Mr. Hunnicutt, if columns are so offensive to Mr. Dennison, then he need only have told me that politely, and I would never use that format again."

"I never knew that you found columns offensive, Dennison?" Mr. Hunnicutt asked his colleague, clearly exhausted from the absurdity of this all.

"It is also a matter with her handwriting," Dennison protested. "It is too—"

"Female?" came a voice behind us. We turned to the doorway, and Mr. Hanley was standing there. "You mean that her writing is too feminine, don't you?"

"Well, I stand by what I said before," Dennison objected.

"You say many things, I gather," Mr. Darcy interjected.

"A female notetaker can be too distracting for the students."

"She stays," Mr. Hanley said simply.

Dennison's eyes narrowed.

"Hanley—"

"She stays," Hanley stated again, so firmly that he would brook no refusal. Seeing that he was greatly outnumbered, Dennison did not relent, but merely retreated.

"Very well. Be it on your heads."

With that, he left.

"Thank you all," I uttered to them.

Instead of showing any sort of obligation or graciousness, Hanley didn't even look at me. But rather, he went over to Hunnicutt's bookshelf, took a book down and began to look through it. Still, without looking to me, he offered instruction.

"You still will be expected to copy your notes for his class, Miss Bennet."

"Yes, sir," I responded.

"And tomorrow, you have my class in the morning. It will be about industrial history. I shall talk slowly and am not averse to columns or particular handwriting. It just has to be clear."

"I shall be prompt, I assure you," I guaranteed. "I was under the impression that I could copy Professor Dennison's notes tomorrow, between sessions."

"Yes, you are correct. Your first day is at an end. Good work."

"Thank you," I replied, uncertain of why he still avoided looking at me. I nodded to Mr. Hunnicutt. "I did not desire for you to undergo any inconvenience of any kind, and I do hope that Professor Dennison will not transfer his bitter feelings toward you both."

"Never fear," Mr. Hunnicutt assured me, "we are not afraid of him."

"Rather," Mr. Hanley responded, still looking through the book and avoiding looking on me, "I daresay it is the other way around."

"Quite so," I deduced. "Well, I shall take my leave."

"If you are amenable to my offering to escort you home," Mr. Darcy suggested, "then would you accept my arm?"

I looked on him and smiled.

"Sir, you may."

He followed me to the coatrack and when I got my coat, he took it from my hands. Looking down on me, his dark and penetrating eyes were softened, and there was a gentleness there that I didn't recall seeing before. It unnerved me, and I barely could attend to my own will.

With such an intense expression, I was able to read his mind. Slowly, he opened my coat, and I placed my arms in the sleeves, and I buttoned it up. He handed me my hat as I put on my gloves and scarf. Out of the side of my eye, I noted that Mr. Hanley had finally turned to us. It was evident that he was confused about the state of our relationship, and perhaps was only apprehensive about what was the mystery that surrounded me.

When I was ready to depart, Darcy offered me his arm, I took it, and we left the hall.

As we walked along the corridors, I suddenly felt bashful. For some reason, I could not look up at Mr. Darcy. Stricken with the recollection of the letter that I had sent him, declining his offer to visit, I could not help but be aware that I had been very foolish. Or maybe I had done right. In the next second, I felt my courage rise against every attempt to be overpowered by self-doubt, and I realized that I owed Mr. Darcy my words, not my silence.

"Mr. Darcy," I breathed heavily, "I thank you for your sudden appearance and in your wonderful ability to assist me in such a manner."

"I had wished to join you on your first day in this hall. I feel fortunate in my time of arrival."

I opened my mouth, then shut it again, at a loss of what to say. Feeling as if my cheeks were flushed, I grew bashful.

"Forgive my shyness," I explained, "I am merely uncertain of what to say."

"You are?"

"Yes," I replied, "I thank you so very much for coming to my defense, and I am much obliged to you. I enjoyed your chivalrous attitude—I do not feel weak by others coming to my defense." His jaw tightened and he looked ahead. "I know that such words might be a little unnerving to you—after all, compliments can be hard to hear sometimes—but you must allow these kind words."

"I do," he replied heavily, "Miss Bennet, you know too well of me to dare presume that I fear your kind words. After all, your good opinion, so little often bestowed, is well worth the earning. When you flatter me, I know that you do not do it falsely, nor do you do it to appeal to my vanity." He looked down on me again and his dark and flashing eyes felt as if they were penetrating into the very depths of my soul. "I know that you do it because you mean it."

"Indeed, I do. I pride myself on fighting my own battles where I may, but I never dismiss when others care enough to support me."

When we exited the hall, a carriage was parked right near the entrance.

"Oh," I laughed, "I should have known that we were not going to be walking anywhere."

"I could not abide having you travel anywhere in any other fashion. Therefore, I opted not to ride my horse through Milton, but chose this mode of transport. I hope that I did not appear too presumptuous."

"You have saved me from a trip on the omnibus," I remarked, my eyes sparkling, "I shall not look a gift horse in the mouth."

Taking his arm, I stepped into the carriage.

"I know that you are aware of where I live," I said, in hushed tones.

"Indeed, I do," Mr. Darcy replied, then he turned to his coachman, "to Frances Street!"

He stepped into the carriage, and we were off.

"This is most fortunate," I began, "this way, the sooner that I get home, the sooner that I can begin to make dinner for my sisters."

Mr. Darcy's eyes widened.

"You cook?"

My stomach felt as if it had sunk to the floor. Feeling my face become flushed, I looked down at my lap. I had grown so comfortable between his coming to my rescue that I had quite lowered my guard.

"Yes, I do," I replied. "You must understand, as I said in my letter, that our reduced circumstances...oh, I am tired of having to explain or feel shame! Mr. Darcy, you know our situation, so perhaps I ought to stop feeling sorry for myself and feeling as if I have to feel embarrassed over it."

"Your circumstances are through no fault of yours," he responded, "but rather is the reaction to the harsh ways of the world. You have nothing to feel sorry over."

Finally, I looked up at him and once more, I saw a softness in his eye.

"Thank you, sir. I suppose that... I should have thought better of you. But you must understand that it was hard upon me, considering our history."

Darcy closed his eyes for a second and then looked out of the window.

"Are you upset with me for speaking so directly?" I asked. "Mr. Darcy, you have to understand that you and I have suffered under miscommunication for too long. I wish to put an end to it."

"I am not upset with you for speaking on such subjects," he insisted. "I am only upset with the impression that I gave you. Or rather, the *reality* of that impression."

"You are referring to the letter I sent in response to your invitation?"

"Yes. I must have given you a horrid notion of my meanness toward families whose condition in life so decidedly below my own. I really did make you feel as if I was not the sort to converse with people who were beneath me."

"I confess that you did. Since I was beneath you, and you gave me that impression so early into our acquaintance, how else was I to feel? What else was I to do? How could I get on?"

"Yes, I did express a—Miss Elizabeth?" He turned back to me.

I looked on him.

He looked on me.

I had just realized how much we both were so very alone.

We were together.

But we also were very much separate.

"A wide gap of misunderstandings," I uttered.

"Pardon?"

"A wide gap of misunderstandings separates us, doesn't it?"

"Yes, it does."

"You once told me how I willfully misunderstood everybody."

"And you once told me that I had a propensity to hate everybody."

"You were right about me, possibly," I allowed.

"And you were very much right about me," he also confessed.

Our eyes were now locked in each other's gaze.

"There it is," I managed to say.

"What?"

"For just one moment, we did not feel so alone. We were in communion with each other."

"You felt that?"

"Yes."

"I did as well."

Very softly, his lips cracked a little smile. This led to me smiling broadly.

"Well, this is something! You have made me quite forget how disastrous my first day of working had ended."

"And it is time that we spoke of that. You really must be an amanuensis for that horrid fellow, Dennison?"

"Sadly, he is one of the professors that I must play scribe to. How tedious, I declare. My first day had been getting on charmingly, until he had to present himself. This just goes to show that, no matter how much one finds a happy moment, a storm cloud will enter soon after to dampen the experience. Have you ever endured such an experience?"

"Yes, I can honestly declare that I have," he replied gravely, and there was something in his expression that cast a darker hue on his temper.

For a brief moment, I felt as if I could read his thoughts and underneath lay the memory of something horrible. And I wondered if I was right? My impertinence had been known to get me into trouble, but it was always the only way that I could ever discover the truth about things. Oh well, come what may!

"Your face dropped, and your tone grew somber," I noted, "can I hazard to guess that a memory has befallen you?"

"Yes, you are correct. To the point of an arrow hitting the direct target."

"Am I allowed to know why?" I asked. "Or is it a great secret?"

"You may know it," he uttered, "because it is only a secret that we share. I was just thinking of my disastrous proposal to you."

You may very well understand my astonishment!

To hear him refer to our painful history, so directly and so frankly, was disarming. However, I should not have been surprised, come to think of the matter, for it was always his way.

"I have upset you," he noted.

"No."

"I think that I must have. Your cheeks have reddened. I have aggravated you. Miss Bennet, please understand that I did not intend to corner you in my carriage and force the memory on you."

"You startled me, that is all. And I know that you did not take me prisoner, in your company, to seek revenge on me. Nor should I have been very alarmed, for as you once told me, you believe in the absolute truth. Now how could I have forgotten that? In fact, I am happy that you have mentioned it."

"You are?"

"Yes. This way, I need not be uneasy any longer. You really must understand that, after what we underwent, it is usually hard to be in each other's company. I'd much rather we confront what has occurred between us, so that awkwardness can end. Or do you fear my forwardness?"

His eyes twinkled.

"I think you would know me too well, to know that I am incapable of respecting the direct approach to such matters. When last we parted in the South, you despised me. Things have changed."

"I wish to assure you that I do not do it for any mercenary reasons, or because my unfortunate circumstances have led to me trying to cater to your good opinion only for the sake of enhancing my position in society. I do not do that at all."

"I know that you do not do that. I would never think it of you."

"Thank you, Mr. Darcy. When I came to Milton, I had no notion of you even being here."

"I know. And I was unaware of your presence here as well, until I saw your sister."

"Yes. Jane told me about that. Oh, how much that must've taken you aback. To turn a corner and see her there."

"Oh, yes. I was very much insecure when facing her."

Rather than confront him again about the fact that he separated Jane from Mr. Bingley, who would have married her, I thought it best to avoid the subject—for the moment.

"When it comes to my change in seeing you," I elaborated, "well, the explanation is not so very simple, but it also *is simple.* First, time heals all arguments. And second, I was not born for ill humor, so I do not like remaining in such a state. Being perpetually angry is no way to live, and I don't know how to live like that. Nor do I want to."

"Then...you do not wish to talk of that most painful day?"

I raised an eyebrow.

"Do you wish to?"

"I feel that I need to. If we do not, then we shall be avoiding issues that ought to be discussed. And that will do no credit for either of us."

I thought on the matter and saw the logic of it.

"Very well, you are correct. First, we must speak of my sister, and your view on her."

"Yes, it would be best."

"You said that you did everything in your power to separate Mr. Bingley from my sister."

"Then this will give me the chance to elaborate on the matter."

I was reserved and was prepared for anything—as well as being prepared for debating everything.

"Mr. Darcy, I do not deny that this brings my past feelings back to the surface. I am feeling the resentment that I felt before."

"I beg you would give me leave before those emotions overtake you."

"Very well, I am prepared. But I warn you in advance, that I will argue, when I see the occasion for it."

"I suppose that is fair."

"More than fair," I replied, saucily.

"When I separated Mr. Bingley from your sister, it was not done primarily due to our difference in situation."

"Was it not?"

"No. My main problem with the match was that I did not believe that your sister loved my friend."

My eyes widened.

"What?"

"I paid close attention to them whenever they spoke together, and I noticed that his affection was much deeper than hers."

"How could you access that?"

"Because, as an outside observer, it is true. While Miss Bennet did receive Bingley's attentions, with pleasure, it was also in so subdued a manner, so sedate a fashion, that she gave no indication of having any particular regard for him. It led me to believe that her heart was not likely to be touched. I thought she liked him, but I did not believe that she was in love with him. I didn't want Bingley to attach himself to a woman that did not possess his same feelings of attachment."

"Mr. Darcy, you are mistaken. She felt so very deeply for him, to the point where she was taken with him from their very first meeting at the assembly."

"Miss Bennet, I mean no offense when I ask this, but I must...do you speak as an objective observer, or as the person who favors her sister and wants her to make a fortunate alliance?"

"Sir, you offend me."

"I do not wish to. Please understand, I speak as a man who wants to protect his friend."

"And that alone is what is having me refrain from my temper being ignited. In the service of a friend is always a genuine excuse. But as you wonder if I do things by being blinded by my loyalty to Jane, you can also be blind to your loyalty to your friend."

Suddenly, I had a thought! As soon as I had it, Charlotte Lucas's face came to my mind. It made me start and grab my waist to steady myself.

"Are you ill?" Mr. Darcy asked me.

"No, pray, it is not that. It is just...sometimes, you experience the effects of having your thoughts and views too quickly overturned."

I tapped my hands against the windowpane, seeing Milton roll along past us.

"Could it be..." I began, bare under the weight of revelation, "that we both might have been blind in some way? Do you remember my friend, Charlotte Lucas?"

"Of course. Miss Charlotte of Lucas Lodge."

"Yes. I can repeat her words because they are in her favor. When we began to see that Jane and Mr. Bingley preferred each other's company, she advised me that Jane's disinterested manner would not be beneficial. She said that if a woman conceals her affection from the object of it, she may lose the opportunity of fixing it. In nine cases out of ten, it would be better to show more affection than she felt, and not less, if she was to secure him. She noted that Bingley liked Jane enormously but would not do more if she did not help his admiration on. For very few of us have the ability to be really in love without proper encouragement."

"She spoke thus?"

"Yes, she did."

"She was right, Miss Elizabeth. Miss Lucas was very much correct. For, having watched them, I discerned no particular regard, and since Charlotte Lucas noticed this, evidently, I am not alone in this matter."

"No," I admitted, "you are not. At the time, I said that Jane did help Bingley on, in the best that her character could allow. I thought that, if Mr. Bingley did not perceive her adoration of him, then he was a fool. But maybe, indeed, I was looking through the lens of a lady who knew her sister's nature and forgot that others did not."

"Then...you are beginning to understand me?"

"Perhaps I am. Logic would have me so. However, as the sister of the woman who you had separated from your friend, will you at least own to the fact that I am more acquainted with her character than you shall be? She cares deeply, but with great strength of feeling, she lets her emotion rest in her soul and doesn't often speak of it. But she speaks to me. Her bashfulness perhaps does render her indifferent in appearance, but I promise that still waters run deep with her. She was in love with Mr. Bingley, sir. She still is."

Mr. Darcy scratched his chin and then he tapped his finger against the glass of the window.

"You do not know what to say, do you?" I asked.

"No, I do not."

"I do not either."

He turned back to me.

"We make a fine pair, don't we?"

"Yes, we do." I chuckled.

My sudden reversal of temper made his eyes soften again. That was a good thing.

The carriage stopped and we arrived at Frances Street.

Now that we were home, I grew apprehensive all over again.

"I thank you, Mr. Darcy," I rushed out, "I appreciate your kindness."

"Miss Bennet," he voiced, "we must talk of your letter to me."

I felt my body stir, filled with internal confusion and consternation.

"Yes?"

"Your point was appreciated because you did not disguise your feelings. You are afraid to invite me in, because you are worried about how I will view your reduced circumstances—especially since I did once rail at the importance of your connections and the status of your family."

"Yes. I never apologized for my family's position in society, and never will. However, when you see our home, I fear that your past preferences will waken and you... I don't want you to be prejudiced of me because of my life now. We are learning to become agreeable to each other. I fear anything that would set us backwards."

"Miss Elizabeth..."

"I do not mean to be so forward in this manner, but it is better for you to know what I feel."

"I would rather you did tell me these truths," he overrode me. "I do prefer us to be honest with each other on such matters. You were not ashamed of your family's situation when your parents were alive, but now, you feel the shame of how you have fallen."

"I am, somewhat. I cannot help it."

"And I do not deny that, once, I was guilty of such a way of thinking. But it is not your fault how your lives ended up, nor will I hold it against you. Your home is your home, and I will not object to it. This will give me the chance to put my new way of thinking to the test. If you invite me inside, then I can prove myself. Miss Bennet, let me do so."

Seeing that there was nothing for it, I agreed.

"Very well," I said, smiling. "Far be it from me to not give you a chance."

He stepped out of the carriage and then helped me down.

Just in that particular moment, dirty chimney sweeps, and factory workers were walking to their homes and Darcy got a wide view of this dirty and filthy street. No one on the street was particularly clean and that was how things were.

Seeing Frances Street made Mr. Darcy even colder in his look, but his whole position and status made him appear like a duck out of water.

Not wishing for him to suffer being such a definite object for all to gawk at, I went to the door, unlocked it, and invited him inside.

Mr. Darcy's eyes were still wide, taking in the destitution of the street for which I now lived. And if his face was any indication of how he felt...he was not happy. Not in the slightest.

"Hullo, Miss Elizabeth!" Mrs. Boucher called from her doorway. She had one of her children in her hand, and her hair fell down the sides of her face, stringy.

"Good day, Mrs. Boucher!" I called back. "I've got an extra side of pork that I'll bring around later."

"Thank yer!" she called, taking a look at Mr. Darcy before she went back into her house. Mr. Darcy watched her progress.

After the second time of me calling his name, Darcy came to, and then he entered my home.

"Mrs. Boucher has six children," I explained. "They never have enough food."

Since it was later in the day, and the sun was setting, and dusk was on the horizon, my house was dark.

"Forgive me," I said, "but I must light some candles."

"Very well," he said, barely paying attention to me. Moving around the room, I brought enough light for Mr. Darcy to see myself and the house in clarity.

"Well," I finalized, trying to be very inviting. "Welcome to my humble abode. The home that has reluctantly become such. I apologize that we do not have enough candles or a parlor and..."

I trailed off when I saw his face. It appeared as if someone had slapped him on the cheek. He moved along the furniture and scrutinized every aspect of what lay before his observations. While he did not say a word, his face said it all. He took in the walls, our attempt to conceal the plain floor with our rugs, the smallness of our lodgings, and the bright-colored upholstery to mask the drabness of every other aspect of our home.

If I had not gathered my courage, indeed, I would have been humbled. At last, he turned back to me, horrified.

"This is how you live?" he asked.

"We must. But we have done our best. We are proud of our attempts. This is all we have."

"If you had married me, you would not have had to suffer this!"

This declaration made me entirely overcome. I had not expected him to speak so.

"If you had married me, I could have spared you of this fate," he continued on, much like a runaway cart. "I could have saved you and your sisters." He took a step toward me. "And I wouldn't have to see you all so unhappily ruined!"

"Mr. Darcy," I uttered, and that did the trick. He blinked and recovered. Remembering himself, he immediately began to grow ashamed.

"Forgive me," he apologized. "Forgive me! I will not remain here now and torment you. Or torment myself, for that matter."

With that, he left my house eagerly. I went after him, but he climbed into his carriage with alacrity and drove off before I could say farewell.

Chapter 16

The Way We Live Now

I was left to stand in the doorway, feeling thoroughly hard on myself. What was I to do? After all, he had uttered things that were the actions of a man who lost control and all sense of propriety. Yet, the words came out of him, and I could not begrudge him—for it was evident that if he didn't say them, his spirit might burst. Sometimes, no matter how contradictory to our logic, we have to speak from our passions.

Closing the door when I saw his carriage drive off, ignoring the chimney sweeps who spied his abrupt departure and clearly were whispering about it amongst themselves, I sat down and pondered what had just occurred.

What was even more shocking was that I did not detest hearing the mention of his proposal. There was a time where the idea of it overwhelmed me and made me wish to ignore him. But now, I wasn't against the mention of it, or the pouring out of his sensibilities.

For a moment, I wondered if I was committing avarice, because my adapting to the subject didn't occur until after I had lost both my parents and became destitute. As such, his wealth and position in society would render him more attractive.

Next, I dismissed that idea immediately. If I cared for his

wealth, I would have been more direct with myself about it, would have deliberated and been more contemplative. But no, these thoughts had never occurred to me at all. Therefore, his pocketbook did not influence me. It was merely a fortunate addition to his character.

Despite that I would never forget his treatment toward Mr. Wickham, I acknowledged, in the depths of my soul, that I was grateful for his love for me. It was flattering. Perhaps that was what I was feeling. I was feeling gratitude. And that did mean something.

I was interrupted from my musings when I heard laughter. The front door suddenly opened and Kitty and Raspberry burst in, laughing about something.

Their bursting in made me jump up like a jack in the box!

"Lizzy," Kitty replied, gurgling merrily, "you will not believe what has happened!"

"It was when we were cleaning one man's hotel room," Raspberry added, closing the door behind me, "and he neglected to mention that he was sleeping late and having a laying in."

"He also...apparently sleeps naked."

My eyes widened, seeing the end of this story.

"Really?" I remarked, putting on my cooking apron. "What happened?"

"Well," Raspberry replied, removing her coat, and slinging it over one of the chairs that she was about to sit down on, "you must imagine our shock when Kitty and I walked in to start changing the sheets and there he was! He woke up, saw us, and I never saw a man move so quickly."

"He just jumped out of the bed, in all of his glory," Kitty cried, taking off her bonnet, "and he just stood there in front of us."

"Did you both run out of the room?" I asked.

Kitty and Raspberry gave each other a look. A look that I could read so very easily.

"You didn't!" I gasped. "You both didn't!"

"We couldn't help it. No one prepares you for that sort of situation."

"By rights of modesty, we ought to have run," Raspberry admitted, "but we were so surprised that we just stood there... staring at him."

"It was like we were transfixed. And then," Kitty said, grabbing my hand, "what do you think? He spoke to us. But not telling us to get out."

"What could he have possibly had to say other than that?" I asked.

"He said..." and here, they both spoke in unison, "'care to join me?'."

They both laughed and fell into their seats.

"I can't believe that!" I scoffed.

"Believe," Kitty cried. "Believe, he asked us to join him."

"You said no, I presume?"

"I don't think we did," Raspberry realized, "rather, I do believe he got the hint, because that's when we decided to run out of the room."

"Yes," Kitty stressed, "finally, we remembered that we had feet."

"I can't believe this! I can't believe..." slowly I began to chuckle. "Truly, I can't believe that... that..." Unable to contain my mirth, I began to laugh as well. So hard that my sides felt as if they were splitting, so I sat down. We had been merry so loudly, that we didn't even hear Jane unlocking the door and coming in.

"I'm home!" she cried when she entered, but then quieted down when she saw us all sitting there, laughing hysterically. "Oh, what is so comical?"

"Kitty and Rasby saw a man in the nude," I chuckled.

"What? How? And no! I've only been gone for three days!"

This made us laugh all the harder.

Kitty and Raspberry told Jane the story while I began to make dinner. Since I had cooked some beef the night before, it had not rotted yet, so I was able to make our meal within an hour's time.

Raspberry was staying for dinner, but there was enough food. What was surprising, however, was when I put her bowl down in front of her.

"What is this?" she asked.

"It's called spaghetti," I observed. "Wait, have you never seen it before?"

"No, I haven't."

"It's Italian."

"Really?" she asked as we all began to eat. Kitty had to show her how to wrap the noodles around her fork. "I'm eating an Italian dish?"

"Yes, you are."

"We never got around to telling you," Jane said, "for a time, we had an Italian cook back at Longbourn."

"Really?"

"Yes. Signora Maria Bertolli was her name, and she was from Florence. The same place as Michelangelo."

"That was how she usually introduced herself," I elaborated, "so that people would be kinder to her. After all, if you're from the same place as one of the most popular artists in history, everyone will look at you less as a stranger and more of a novelty. That did work in her favor. Eventually, people got over her being different."

"I know a little bit about that," Raspberry empathized. "And how did she end up in Hertfordshire?"

"Life," Jane answered. "She married an Englishman, he was a Hertfordshire native, he brought her to England, and she was a leaf along the wind."

"But fate was not friendly to her," Kitty elaborated, as I put pots of water over the fire, so that I could have a bath later. "Two years they were married before he just suddenly popped off."

"He died?"

"Yes. Well, here she was, now entirely alone. This all was right around the time that our cook died. Not ready to return to Florence, she appealed to our mother and father to fill the post. We tried her out, liked her food and we took her on. Foreign cooks are the best, and Maria was wonderfully fussy. She complained about us sisters not being able to cook."

"To be fair, she was right," I stated. "She always used to say that knowing how to cook, even simply, was one more step toward independence and freedom. Imagine if we had no idea how to cook? We'd have been lost!"

I looked at Raspberry, worried that she wouldn't like it. But she did!

"I'm eating an Italian dish," she remarked. "I never thought that would happen."

"Well," I boasted, "wait till you try my lasagna and ravioli. That's the best."

"What's lasagna and ravioli?"

"Oh!" Jane and Kitty cried, merrily. "You cannot imagine!"

After I delivered the side of pork to the Bouchers, I was ready to begin my evening routine.

Since none of us had the time or ability to boil too much water, we had to share baths. Jane and I went first and were sitting there, in the washbasin, bathing ourselves quickly. The reason for this was because, sadly, we didn't have the ability to waste water. Once we were done, Kitty and Raspberry had to go into the very same water that Jane and I had just used.

This fact only brought me closer to accepting the new circumstances to my life. Individual baths belonged to the life that we used to have. Shared baths, with recycled water, was the life that we now were in.

And even more, Mr. Darcy's parting words hit me harder.

"Does Raspberry usually spend the night?" I asked Jane as we washed ourselves.

"Yes. Normally it's when I am living with the Kirkpatricks. It keeps Kitty from being alone in the house when I'm gone. But even if I wasn't away for gaps of time, she sometimes would still spend the night. Sometimes, she and Kitty get so wrapped up in their conversations, that they don't pay attention to the time. It's better that Raspberry doesn't walk home so late. Too dangerous for her."

"Oh, I see. How did she and Kitty become friends, I wonder?"

"It's simpler than you think. When Lydia and Kitty had to separate, Kitty needed a lively friend who clung to her, and Raspberry needed a friend who wasn't tyrannical. Both of them found each other and now they are inseparable."

We finished washing, got out of the water, dried ourselves off and told Kitty and Raspberry that we were done. When we opened the washroom door, Kitty and Raspberry rushed in, removed their towels, jumped into the washbasin, and began to splash each other.

"Remember, girls," Jane instructed, "if you get into a water fight, you have to clean it up."

"Yes, mum," Kitty replied, and they quieted down and bathed.

Later that night, Jane and I were lying in bed.

"I saw Mr. Darcy today," I uttered in the darkness.

"You did?" I heard Jane roll over and face me, for I had been staring at the wall.

"Yes."

"What did he say?"

"He protected me from a pernicious fellow employee, escorted me home, saw how we lived, remarked on how I would not have to live such a way if I had accepted him, then left, embarrassed that he had said such."

"Elizabeth, I am sure that he did not mean it in an offensive way."

"He didn't," I rushed out. "Do not fear. I am not in the mood to misunderstand him tonight. Quite frankly, I don't have the energy for it. No. I understand what he meant. He was sorry that he could not protect me from all of this."

"And what do you feel about that?"

"I cannot marry a man who I am not in love with. But I do not deny that I was very flattered that he still cares. I suppose, in that moment, I was happy. And perhaps I was sad that I was happy about it."

"Life and love...are very confusing."

"Yes. They both are."

I fell asleep.

Chapter 17

The Correction

O nce Mr. Darcy had gotten back to his hotel room, he was resolved.

He could not leave Milton! No, he must stay! From his experience with Mr. Dennison, to seeing the state of Frances Street. He could not leave Miss Elizabeth alone in this dreadful place.

Even though she had rejected his proposal, he could not deny the pleasure of seeing her, nor could he abide knowing he left her to remain not fully safe. She did not ask him to help her, and she never would. However, he flattered himself that she would understand why he did anyway.

However, he couldn't remain in the hotel forever, so it perhaps would be best for him to rent an establishment eventually. The next day, he would visit Thornton and ask him what the best way would be to find proper lodgings to rent from anyone.

Next, he dismissed the idea, in place of a better one that he felt that he should have identified earlier.

After coming to that resolution, it now came time for him to set all his other affairs in order. Tomorrow, he would have his valet, Jefferson, compose letters to his housekeeper, Mrs.

Reynolds, to understand that he would not return to Pemberley as he had expected. Next, they would have to write to his Aunt, Lady Catherine de Bourgh, to tell her that he would remain in the North for a longer duration.

The last two letters were not ones that he ought to have his valet compose but were now his responsibility.

Sitting down, he wrote a letter to his sister, Georgiana, who was staying in town with her friends. She needed to know where he was and why his plans had been changed. He also wondered if she would wish to visit him there, for the sake of a change of scene and society. For wherever Mr. Wickham was in the world, it definitely was NOT in the North. If she came, he knew that she would at least enjoy knowing that she wouldn't encounter a man who almost destroyed her life.

The last letter to write had to have been the harder one.

For this one required him to confront his own error and guilt. This one required more weight behind his words and more deliberation on how things ought to be phrased. At some point, he had to get up and eat some dinner to refresh himself before he continued, to gather his wits again.

At last, he finished his letter, near the midnight hour. Prepared, at last, he rubbed his eyes and read it over.

Dear Bingley,

I write to you as a friend, who needs to reconcile himself with the actions of his past. More important, I come to you as a man who has to confront an error that may have been made.

I just acknowledge that I start at the end, rather than the beginning. Allow me to correct that.

As you know, I am visiting an acquaintance of mine here in Milton, Mr. John Thornton, manufacturer and magistrate. When coming, I was surprised to discover mutual friends of ours: the Bennet sisters of Longbourn.

Or rather, three of the five. Miss Mary Bennet remains

in town, working for her uncle, a Mr. Gardiner. The youngest, Miss Lydia, is married to an officer, Denny— which is not wholly unexpected, when we analyze her character.

However, the other three sisters, Miss Jane Bennet, Miss Elizabeth, and Miss Kitty, are living here, in the North. Miss Kitty is a chambermaid to The King's Hotel, Miss Elizabeth is a professional notetaker to a Granger Hall, where classes are held. And Miss Jane Bennet...is a governess to a family named Kirkpatrick. They are now women of profession.

I am aware that this will come as a surprise to you, for you are not aware of their present situation.

And here is where one of my many sins must come to light.

This sin is withholding information that you had the right to know of.

As you know, the Bennets cousin is Mr. Collins, and my aunt is his patroness. Well, she wrote to me a few months ago, to inform me that she was seeking a new reverend for her parish, since Mr. Collins now had become a gentleman who owned Longbourn.

Naturally, when hearing this, I wrote to her to elaborate on the matter.

Over time, I would learn everything. Mr. and Mrs. Bennet passed away in a carriage accident, thus leaving all five sisters orphaned, and with little to live on. At this time, Lydia married Denny, to save herself from destitution and from being unprotected.

Since Mr. Collins had been recently married, he natu- rally was all too eager to take possession of Longbourn. Having to relieve his post, he placed him and his new wife in Longbourn, as their new master and mistress very quickly.

The Bennet sisters were encouraged to find another

place to live. Until they were ready to find employment, they were homeless. Mr. Collins wrote back to Lady Catherine about how they were staying with their aunt and uncle, the Philips, or the Gardiners. Once they all found employment, they scattered in different directions. I lost track of their whereabouts.

When coming to Milton, I found out what happened to them. And that is how I found them here.

Bingley, to see them thus... I am humbled. I had wronged them. I know this now.

More importantly, I have recently begun to entertain the fact that I misjudged the state of your relationship with Miss Bennet. You know how I watched you and Miss Bennet most acutely and observed how her affection for you was not as deep as yours. All that I saw was a woman who did not love you in the way that you loved her. Believe me, I was doing my best to save you from heartbreak, or from being ensnared by a woman who was choosing you for your wealth, and not for your character.

Since my coming to Milton, I have made a further acquaintance with Miss Elizabeth. The more that I have spoken with her, the more that I discovered that I willfully misunderstood Miss Bennet's nature. She is not indifferent, as I had determined. Rather, she may perhaps just be somewhat shy, and is averse to exposing her feelings to the eyes of the world.

When it comes to securing a person's heart, I do not regard this as being the best plan on Miss Bennet's part, but that is her right to be so.

Thus, Bingley, I lay my truth before you and I apologize for what I have done. If you can forgive me, perhaps we can set about repairing any injuries that I may have inflicted.

Would you come to Milton? Would you come to see Miss Bennet?

If you do, please write back to me as soon as possible to inform me of when you shall come. The sooner that you arrive, the better it shall be.

F.D.

The next morning, Darcy had Jefferson send the letter by express, hoping to hear from Bingley soon.

Chapter 18

Settling In

The next day, we all woke up, got dressed, ate our breakfast, and went to work.

When arriving at Granger Hall, I was met immediately by Mr. Hunnicutt.

"Did you hear of this new professor in our midst?" he asked. "He is a former clergyman of some sort, who left his profession, uprooted his family from the South and have decamped to this town. Now, he has joined our staff, and will teach a range of classes that include ecclesiastic architecture."

"Would he, by any chance, be a Mr. Hale from Helstone?" I asked, removing my bonnet, coat, and scarf, to prepare for the day.

"You do know of him? Oh, and I was very much hoping to be the one to give you the news."

"You have been beaten for weeks. I knew this because I traveled to Milton with them. Mr. Hale's daughter is one of my closest friends, so I am well acquainted with Mr. Hale."

"Oh. What sort of man is he?"

"You may set your heart at rest. He is a very kind and steady man."

"But to uproot his entire family and move to Milton, is very strange behavior."

"It was a matter of conscience. There were certain things that he was ordered to do that he did not believe in."

"Such as?"

"I will say no more than that," I refused to elaborate, "for that is his story to tell. But I would not have any negative word spread about them. Everyone has the right to change their lives and make a new way for themselves when they are being true to their principles."

"You think me to be a gossip?"

"I think no such thing, Mr. Hunnicutt," I said, removing my portable desk, "I just know that you are curious. In the same fashion that everyone is in this world. But I will not leave you in suspense and would rather set your mind at ease. He is a gentle man who was not thrown out from his home and cast onto an industrial town. He walked away from something of his own choosing, out of desire to make his own life. After all, don't we all want to be free eventually?"

"I suppose so. Or perhaps he's reached that stage in his life that most men undergo."

"What?"

"Sometimes, a man reaches a time in his life where he questions everything around him, wondering where he was going and where he hasn't been. And then he is stricken by some sort of crisis, where he realizes that he has not had a large effect on the world, and he must change that. So, he gets up, he gets out, and he has this dramatic shift. Some men act on it. Other men don't. And then there are the other men."

"And what do those men do?"

"Drink. Then they dream. Then they drink again. Then they dream again."

I laughed.

"That's how men are like?"

"Oh, you have no idea. Every now and again, we men reach

an age where there's a chance that we get stricken by some sort of crisis, and we must change who we are."

"I suppose, no matter how hard I try, I will never fully understand the minds of man."

"We are an ancient race. But that does not make us any easier or difficult to comprehend over time."

"So, who am I taking notes for today?" I asked.

"Mr. Hanley."

I was apprehensive and Hunnicutt noticed.

"What is that look for?"

"Well, yesterday he had to be put into an awkward position of defending me against his fellow professor. When you owe a person that much, it can be discomforting."

"Never fear, he will act like it never happened. I'd advise you to do the same."

"Really?"

"It's the best thing you can do for him. We live in a world where gratitude can embarrass people."

"Do you ever notice how backwards that is?"

"Oh yes. Every gray-colored day."

Mr. Hanley taught two classes in one day. This was as a result of his popularity in subject matter. Hanley also specialized in the history of engineering and technological advancement. What was even more important was his ability to understand his subject matter. He didn't just list things, but rather, he clearly had a knowledge of how the technology worked. The first class was focused on the railway system, starting with the very first engineer to design the initial models. He also touched on the resistance that was met when the railway system was adapted into culture. Not just from the British perspective, but also the non-British one. Trains were something that all cultures were a little hesitant to engage in.

"Those who look forward to technological advancement and achievement were eager for the railroad system to be adapted into their cultures," he finalized, "but others feared the repercussions of humanity moving too quickly. Thus, it presents the fact of life...even when progress will help humanity move forward, people will always fear the most inevitable and forever moving thing: change. It drives fear in them that we all cannot imagine. Anything that lends itself toward the different, the unfamiliar, will be met with resistance. After all, to coin a phrase: the devil you know is better than the devil you don't. Technology, in this century, has proven that no matter how fast humanity goes, no matter how far we drive ourselves, we WILL persevere. The evolution of engineering can be regarded as a metaphor for the evolution of man. It will happen. Therefore, what does this tell you? Sometimes change is for the better and you must support it. Sometimes change is for the worse and you must fight it. Don't fear all change ignorantly. History has a way of punishing such prejudice. See change for what it is, and when others fear it, do not hate them. Give them time to catch up to you. Be like the train: move forward and when people are ready to get on, let them on and take them and they'll go where they are needed. Here ends the lesson."

The students clearly admired him.

His next class was on the engineering of recorded sound. It focused on the evolution of the phonautograph, which was the earliest known device for recording sound. Previously, tracings had been obtained of the sound-producing vibratory motions of tuning forks and other objects by physical contact with them, but not of actual soundwaves as they propagated through air or other mediums. It was invented by Frenchman Édouard-Léon Scott de Martinville, and was patented on March 25, 1857. It transcribed sound waves as undulations or other deviations in a line traced on smoke-blackened paper or glass.

When I had took notes for his first class, he never even bothered to look at it. But at the end of the second class, he came up to me to analyze my work. When he did, his tone was simple and direct.

"That will do."

I knew that was his way of an intense compliment.

"Thank you. You are a very good instructor. Your students love you."

"Oh," he replied, growing bashful. Removing his spectacles, he rubbed his eyes, nervous. "Well, um—thank you."

Typical! He really had no idea how to take a compliment.

"Uncle Virge!"

We turned and it was little Molly Gibson[1].

With a chaperone behind her, she had entered the hall apprehensively. When I turned to her, her face brightened up.

"Molly!" I said, jumping up. Seeing my approachable manner, she rushed up to me. Surprised at her eagerness, I laughed. Bending down on the floor, I opened my arms and she rushed into them, wrapping her hands around my neck.

I picked her up and held her.

"And how do you do today, little one?" I asked.

"I woke up today with a stomachache."

"Oh, you poor thing. Does it still hurt?"

"It's better now, thank you."

"I hate it when I have to wake up to that feeling. That and headaches."

"I hate those too. And toothaches."

"Oh, those are the worst!"

I was prepared to set her down to get my desk, but Mr. Hanley had done it for me. Seeing both of us looking so happy,

---

1. Molly Gibson is named after the heroine from Elizabeth Gaskell's other main novel: Wives and Daughters.

he offered to carry all my belongings back to the office while I carried little Molly along the way.

As I followed behind him, Molly told me about how she almost made a friend this week, but she never saw the child again. When I asked if she had any children her age to play with, she said that she had none.

When we exited the hall, we were met by Margaret Hale, who had come to meet me there.

"Look, Molly," I remarked, "Margaret comes to see us."

"Miss Hale!" Molly laughed.

"Molly," Margaret greeted her. "We meet again."

I set Molly down and egged her on.

"Run to Margaret," I encouraged, "go on. Fe fi fo fum!"

Molly ran to Margaret, who picked her up and held her as well.

"And how does the little princess do?" Margaret asked.

"I'm not a princess," Molly replied.

"Yes, you are."

"Really? Uncle Virge, did you hear? I'm a princess."

"Yes," Mr. Hanley replied, bashful. "Yes, you are."

We escorted them to Mr. Hanley's office. I put everything away, we said farewell to the uncle and his niece and left for home.

Chapter 19

Bad Second Impression

"So," I began as Margaret and I walked along, "how does your mother and Dixon do? Are they still angry at the world?"

"I love mother and Dixon, but they are still grumbling. Yet, I understand mama's reaction to things. She has reached that part of her life where she cannot adjust to this new environment."

"This does seem like a town for a person who was taught to have energy."

"Precisely. Do you have time to come and see our new home on Crampton?"

"You all really did choose that place?"

"Yes, despite the bad memories that it brings up. I swear, I never wish to see that Mr. Thornton again in the whole course of my life."

We talked about my day, and my experiences so far, the entire way to Canute Street, Crampton. When we got there, we entered her new home and Margaret called out through the house.

"Father, Mother and Dixon!" Margaret called as we began to remove our coats, placing them on the coatrack. "Elizabeth has come to visit, but she can't stay long."

"Oh, Margaret!" Mr. Hale's voice called. "In here. Bring Elizabeth with you."

He had been calling us from a parlor on the left.

We had removed our hats and entered the study. When we did, Mr. Hale was standing by his desk, and I saw how the room had been fitted properly to his taste. But he was not alone. There was a man sitting opposite him and his back was to us.

"Elizabeth," Mr. Hale greeted me warmly, "welcome to our new home. Margaret, I am very excited to introduce you to my friend and first proper pupil."

The man stood up and turned to us. When seeing him, Margaret and I were both alarmed and I sensed our jaws dropping rather than them actually doing so.

"This is Mr. John Thornton," Mr. Hale introduced, his voice still animated.

There, before us, was Mr. John Thornton, Master of Marlborough Mills, the man who ordered us out of his factory when we saw him abusing his past employee.

When he had first stood up to see us, Mr. Thornton's face was casual, complacent, and even pleasant. But when he began to recognize us and took in the lack of our enthusiasm when seeing him, his face changed to one of silent resignation.

"Mr. Thornton," Mr. Hale continued, "this is my daughter, Margaret, and her friend, Miss Elizabeth Bennet."

"Actually," Mr. Thornton replied, diplomatically, "your daughter, her friend, and I have already become acquainted."

"Yes," Margaret responded, her tone severe, "we have."

Mr. Thornton leaned forward, his eye keen as he felt her quiet disdain.

"I can imagine that I did not offer the best first impression," Mr. Thornton explained, "but you came upon me when I had to dismiss one of my workers."

"Did you have to dismiss him in such a violent way?" Margaret questioned. "What was the meaning for casting blows on such a weaker character than yourself?"

"Yes," I supported, "sir, that is a frightening tendency of yours. Do you have a temper?"

"Ladies..." Mr. Hale interrupted, unsettled to see us berate Mr. Thornton, even if our questions were just and calmly spoken.

"I do not deny, Mr. Hale," Mr. Thornton acknowledged, "that your daughter and Miss Bennet are somewhat correct. I do, indeed, have a temper. Yet, it was provoked by a worker who earned his dismissal, as well as my anger."

"Your anger?" Margaret echoed.

"Yes, Miss Hale, my anger."

"What excuse are you about to give?"

"Margaret!" Mr. Hale reprimanded, but Mr. Thornton rolled on past him.

"The excuse of an employer who gave the worker three warnings, and he wasted all of them for frivolous and dangerous purposes. The worker had been warned for when he smoked in the sorting room, which could have led to fire and the costing of many innocent lives and machinery, and twice he was negligent at the spinning and weaving, and he could have broken the machines that he was employed to treat with care. From my income to my fellow workers, I have their care to consider, and when they are ever endangered by the actions of one, I will remove that one, by ANY means necessary. I gave him his chance, and he failed to do the correct thing repeatedly."

Margaret and I were silenced by this, but not out of blind obedience. It is merely that whenever you hear another perspective, you must consider it. Yet, neither she nor I were ready to be submissive, for we did not forget how he spoke to us, when his temper was flared.

"I should go," Mr. Thornton said abruptly, seeing that his visit was better to end. He put on his hat and turned to Mr. Hale. "I shall have my mother and sister call on you."

"My wife would look forward to their visit," Mr. Hale

assured Thornton. "And by all means, we look forward to any visit of yours. Don't we, Margaret?"

We all turned to Margaret. However kindred our spirits were in this case, I was not a resident, so she couldn't rely upon me to speak. It was not my place.

Margaret managed to raise her eyes to Mr. Thornton, who returned her gaze with a fierce look of his own.

"My father looks forward to your visit," she allowed, "therefore, it is a pleasure to become acquainted with your family. And I am happy to see that he has made friends."

Mr. Thornton blinked, a little uncertain of how to receive her last response. Then Margaret continued.

"I do not agree with your methods," she uttered, "and perhaps I never will. But your story is your own. That I will acknowledge. But my views are mine as well."

"I get the feeling that we shall be at odds very often," Mr. Thornton predetermined.

"Time will tell," Margaret finalized.

He bowed to us both.

"Miss Hale, Miss Bennet. And Mr. Hale."

Mr. Hale saw his new friend out. Margaret and I stood there.

"I cannot like him, Elizabeth," Margaret whispered to me. "I cannot."

Soon, we were joined by Mr. Hale.

"Margaret?" Mr. Hale questioned. "I am happy that you did your best to be kinder by the end, but I do believe that you could have been gentler in your tone."

"I am sorry, Father. I did not mean to offend your friend. However, you weren't there when Lizzy and I first met him. You didn't see the side of him that we saw. You don't know what he's like."

"He explained himself."

"I saw. But I also know what I know." Seeing that Margaret had quite made up her mind, Mr. Hale turned to me.

"How was your day, Miss Bennet?"

"Well, thank you," I said. "Nothing of note, but it was altogether, a good day."

He smiled gently at me.

"And how is your day?" I asked. "I see that you have a new student."

"More than one," Mr. Hale furthered. "I have spent the day meeting with several pupils. They came to me recommended by Mr. Bell, but tomorrow, I shall meet more, that are even more the immediate influence of Mr. Thornton. He has recommended me to certain young boys. They are mostly of the age when many boys would be still at school, but, according to the prevalent, and apparently well-founded notions of Milton, to make a lad into a good tradesman he must be caught young, and acclimated to the life of the mill, or office, or warehouse. According to Mr. Bell, if a boy were sent to even the Scotch Universities, he came back unsettled for commercial pursuits."

"How much more so if he went to Oxford or Cambridge, where he could not be entered till he was eighteen?" I asked.

"Very good, yes. So, according to Thornton, most of the manufacturers placed their sons in sucking situations of fourteen or fifteen years of age, unsparingly cutting away all offshoots in the direction of literature or high mental cultivation. They do this in hopes of throwing the whole strength and vigor of the plant into commerce. Yet still there are some wiser parents, and some young men, who have sense enough to perceive their own deficiencies, and strive to remedy them."

"I noticed this when I was taking notes at Granger Hall. Some men do know to better themselves here."

"A natural inclination."

"That I will note and appreciate," Margaret added. "If men in the prime of life, who have the stern wisdom to acknowledge their own ignorance, and to learn late what they should have learnt early, then so much the better."

"Precisely!" Mr. Hale confirmed. "To learn when you are

still a boy, is natural. But to be a grown man and willing to learn something new takes great strength. It goes to show that there will always be exceptions to those who feel that an old dog cannot learn new tricks. So far, Mr. Thornton is my oldest pupil to hand, and I cannot help but like him enormously, Margaret."

"Like I said, I am happy that you have made a new friend, Father. But I still will think of him as I did before. Now, I should tell mama to expect Mrs. Thornton's visit. Come, Elizabeth."

I mentioned Mr. Hale's new position to Granger Hall, complimented him on it, then followed Margaret to her mother's room.

"Well, so ends my desire to have shielded my father from the truth," Margaret uttered to me.

"You had no choice. He was perhaps going to learn it anyway. Besides, it has not shaken his friendship with Mr. Thornton, so your actions have done no harm."

We knocked on the bedroom door and it was answered by Dixon.

"This dirty air in this awful place has made your mother sick at last!" Dixon groaned when we entered. Mrs. Hale was resting in her bed, but she was awake and happy to see us.

"How are you, Dixon?" I asked.

"Sick as well! This time of the year is already trying to anyone, but now this place may be the death of me!"

"I do not think so," I replied, amused. "You are Stonehenge."

"Oh, I better be," Dixon replied.

"Dixon, sit down and rest yourself," Mrs. Hale said to her. "Margaret is here, and I am well. Go and rest, so that you may recover."

"I'd feel terrible leaving you alone."

"I do not want you to work yourself to death."

"I probably will, seeing as how I have no help to speak of. I have to do everything."

"We are having a hard time finding another servant to assist Dixon," Margaret explained as she pulled up chairs for us to sit by Mrs. Hale. "Every time that we interview someone, she shows herself to be unsuitable."

"Or uncouth," Dixon added. "Most of these girls are crude anyway, and I wouldn't let them in the house for my life."

"I have come to a decision," Margaret said, "Dixon, I will help you with the household duties."

"You, Miss?"

"Yes. I'll help you clean, iron and tend to everything."

"You shouldn't be doing that, Margaret," Mrs. Hale objected.

"I must. Very soon, we will have company. I came to tell you about a visit." Margaret turned to Dixon. "Dixon, like mama said, go and rest. You need to recover to save your strength."

"Right, miss."

Dixon left us alone.

"What is this talk about a visit?" Mrs. Hale asked.

"One of father's friends, a Mr. Thornton, has a mother and sister. I don't know the precise day, but over the course of the next two weeks, they will call on us."

"I cannot entertain guests in a house such as this."

"We have gotten better wallpaper, didn't we?"

"Yes. But that doesn't change the fact that this house is most unsuitable for entertaining. And you, Margaret? To be tending to housework!"

"It cannot be helped," Margaret said, "and hopefully, it will not be so terrible. We have to assist where we may. Besides, it is not as if I shall remain a maid all day." She chuckled. "I shall not always be Peggy the laundry-maid, but will always turn into Margaret Hale, the Lady, afterwards."

This was a joke, and Margaret had meant for it to be so.

However, Mrs. Hale did not regard it as such, and actually took the comment seriously.

"Yes."

Mrs. Hale then looked at me, forlorn.

"If anyone had told me when I was Miss Beresford, and one of the belles of the county, that a child of mine would have to stand half a day, in a little poky kitchen, working away like any servant, that we might prepare properly for the reception of a tradesman, and that this tradesman would be the only..."

"Oh, Mama," Margaret objected, "I don't mind ironing, or any kind of work for you and Papa. I am myself a born and bred lady through it all, even though it comes to scouring a floor, or washing dishes."

"I know, and that is why you are so much a godsend," Mrs. Hale assured her, tapping Margaret's hand. "But still, Miss Bennet, this is not what my life was supposed to be like at this point. I would never have seen my daughter having to be this way."

"I suppose, if my mother were here, she would say precisely the same," I empathized.

"Oh, yes," Mrs. Hale said, her eyes widening, "your mother. To see you reduced to this?" Mrs. Hale looked on us both. "Both of us would feel so disappointed in ourselves. This would not be what any mother would want for her child, to see her reduced to a situation that was lesser than what she was born into. We are supposed to end our lives seeing you greater than ourselves, not lesser."

"Mama," Margaret assured her, "do not look on it that way."

"You do the best that you can," I said, "but life will sometimes get in the way. My mother knew that no matter how hard she tried to have us escape that fate."

"As any mother should. *As any mother should.*"

Mrs. Hale closed her eyes.

"You both can enjoy yourselves. I am getting sleepy."

We left her alone.

"Hopefully one day she will grow to get used to living in Milton," I said to Margaret as we walked to her bedroom.

"I hope so, but Lizzy, I am not sure. She never fully accustomed herself to living in Helstone, and that was such a beautiful place. If she could not get used to that beauty, then she might not get used to all this smoke. I think it's change that is hard on her."

"Yes, not everyone is used to adapting. But we must."

"Yes, we must. Elizabeth, I still miss Helstone! I miss it so much!"

Sitting down next to her on her bed, I held her hands.

"And I miss Hertfordshire," I empathized. "I miss Longbourn."

"How will we make it?"

"We just have to. And we will."

"Yes," she said, tapping my hand. "We just have to. And I will. I will."

"You already are."

She smoothed out her dress, went to the window and looked out of it.

I was used to this habit of hers. Whenever she had an emotion that she needed to suppress, or to resolve within herself, she would take a moment to reflect.

It was never for very long, so I was prepared for her to rally, two minutes later.

"Oh," she said at last, turning back to me, "and I forgot. Edith says hullo."

"She wrote to you?"

"Yes, she did." Margaret went to her chest and pulled out a letter from the top of it. "She writes of ideal married life and seeing as how Captain Lennox is always a jovial man, I can very well believe that he is a great husband."

She handed me the letter.

"That I can attest to," I said, taking the paper from her. "Captain Lennox has taught me, in life, that sometimes a person can either be intelligent, or they could be pleasant. He chose to be pleasant. Maybe those are the best sort to marry."

Looking over the letter, I smiled. There was always something about Edith. Her personality was so vibrant that you saw her within her words.

Edith and Captain Lennox had gone to Corfu for their honeymoon. She wrote of the novelty of it, their voyage along the Mediterranean—their music, and dancing aboard the ship. She easily and artlessly unfolded the gay new life opening upon her, her house with its trellised balcony, and its views over white cliffs and the deep blue sea. Edith wrote fluently and well. She did mention me and wondered how I would enjoy this all. But she knew that I did. She even wondered if Captain Lennox's regiment stopped another year at Corfu, that maybe we could come out and visit her there.

At last, I lowered the letter.

"She writes fluently and well."

"She does. Edith's life seems like the deep vault of blue sky above her—free."

"Utterly free from fleck and cloud."

"If the regiment does stay at Corfu for another year, would you go?" Margaret asked me.

"Of course. If my work allowed me to."

"That's the problem. Our lives won't let us have that time away."

"No, it won't. In this moment, more than any other, I do understand why your father did leave the church. There is something to be said for being able to control one's life."

"Yes. I always saw that about the reasons behind his change. However, I just wish that it didn't have to take us far away. To a whole other world, where we have to fight our way through crowds, learn to make new acquaintances from people with different customs, face the gray of everything, and have to mingle with the likes of Mr. Thornton."

"How do you feel that *that* man might very well become Mr. Hale's close friend? Because it does tend to be going in that direction."

"I saw that as well," she replied, putting the letter away. "I think my father was really taken with Mr. Thornton. I saw such admiration in his eyes. But Lizzy, you and I saw what we saw."

"His fiery temper. His violent temper."

"Yes. Even if that man, Custer, was in the wrong, that behavior was too harsh. And the way that he spoke to us was like I was looking into the eyes of a demon. After all, if he behaved that way to ladies, how would he behave toward others? That is the dilemma!"

"After all," I said, "it is only a matter of time before he acts that way again," I observed.

"Precisely. I will accept and try and be polite to him, for Father's sake. I am happy that he has found a friend. But as for the rest, I am determined to think of him as I did before. I cannot ever see myself liking Mr. Thornton."

Since Frances Street was not too far from Crampton, I preferred to walk rather than take the omnibus. The sun was setting and so was the clarity of traveling in such a way.

An intense fog swept over Milton and sometimes you could not see more than four feet in front of you. As such, people would sometimes not appear to you until very suddenly.

Other times, you saw a face here, an arm there, and you would knock into someone by sheer accident. Despite the large number of people on the street, implying that all was safe, you did feel that we were shadows, waifs, or ghosts who were moving amongst each other, not fully knowing or caring of each other's existence.

Chapter 20

Friends 'Till the End

E ventually, I reached Frances Street and was met by Jane, Kitty and Raspberry. They all had a little bit to tell me about their day. The first bit of beneficial news came from Raspberry.

"The regiment will be coming through town tomorrow," she said, "and Plato's letter has proceeded them. He does know of a Mr. Denny, who will be coming to Milton."

"That means Lydia is coming!" Kitty cried merrily. "Raspberry, you will love her."

"But will she love me? That is the question."

"If she doesn't, don't worry," Jane offered, slicing up some bread on the table. "She'll overcome it."

"I'm not so sure about that," I said. "Rasby, Lydia has not always had the ability to get used to things that she doesn't want to. But there surely will be no difference. And what else have you discovered?" I asked, putting on my apron.

"This is the bad news. Plato has not heard of any Mr. Wickham in his militia. If Mr. Wickham is still in the army, then that means that he must now be in a different regiment. Your friend will not be in the army that is coming."

"Very well. His coming is not vital to my happiness. It merely would have been nice to see him. That is all."

"Oh, come now, Lizzy," Kitty crowed. "You know that you were once in love with Mr. Wickham."

"You magnify and augment my emotions too much. I admire him, and greatly enjoy his company. That is all."

"Very well, keep your secrets." She whispered something in Raspberry's ear, and I knew that it was about me. But I didn't mind it. In Milton, my *past* was of no consequence to anyone. There were no impertinent remarks for me to suffer under or critical eyes to be cast on me. That was the joys of being of little consequence in the world; there was no shame to be endured because no one cared about you.

Soon after I had come, Raspberry had to depart, so that it wasn't too late for her to walk home alone.

Now that her attention was more focused, Kitty remembered something.

"Oh, Lizzy! You received a letter today."

"Who is it from?"

"Charlotte Lucas."

"Really?" I asked, amazed. "Letters from Hertfordshire don't always have a habit of being good news."

"Why would you be afraid of a letter from Charlotte?" Jane asked me.

"For no particular reason," I replied, sarcastic, "for what harm could there come from receiving a letter from a longtime friend, who rejected an offer to secure her future, to protect our friendship, and for us to be separate, so she feels like she lost everything out of loyalty?"

"Oh," Kitty remarked, "I see. Well...best to just read it."

I took the letter, opened it up and began to read it while the rice was heating up on the stove.

Charlotte began her letter very sanguinely, and she gave a pleasant portrait of Hertfordshire. Home sounded like home. Naturally, I had no choice but to see the parallel between Charlotte's letter and Edith's when she was happily married in Corfu. They still had the comforts of a pleasant family life, while the rest of us had to toil and suffer the air of the North.

At last, Charlotte's letter took a turn for the inevitable: of living in Hertfordshire and having to endure being in Mr. Collins's presence occasionally...

Dear Lizzy, how you must have suffered when he was vying for your hand!

A proper gentleman would not reduce himself toward revenge in my case, but I believe he has, in the only subtle way that he could. When you had first rejected Mr. Collins's offer of marriage, I was merely being polite and kind towards him, because I sympathized with his position.

Having never had any beauty myself, we humans naturally relate to others who are like us. Mr. Collins has nothing exceptional to his character, from his mind to his face, so I pitied him, while also relating to him. But that really was ALL that there was!

I had no intention of having him think that I thought on him in a romantic way. And it shows, no good deed goes unpunished. But now, things have unfolded in the way that they had no choice but to. He had proposed to me, I had rejected him, he quickly married another woman to save his pride (as father has voiced on more than one occasion) you all lost Longbourn, he inherited it, and now he has become even more conceited. Being landed gentry has fed into his self-assurance, and he has hinted to me, on more than one occasion of my misfortunes for having rejected him.

Lizzy, he is taking revenge on me, and if I were to show any sort of resignation, his revenge would be complete. It is strange—but this all only adds to my resolve. Every day that I am in his company, the more that I am determined how right I was for rejecting him! I could have done my best to have adjusted to marriage to him, but now, I prefer to think that I am better where I am. Even my parents understand my refusal now.

For, as you may recall, our mothers were both alike when they discovered that we both had rejected him. Your mother tried to force you to accept Mr. Collins. My mother tried to influence me. Yet both to no avail.

My father was upset, but soon it gave way to acceptance. Now it has given way to admiration—and the same for mother. They see how Mr. Collins lords his triumph over me, how he evidently does not love his wife, but views her as a sort of trophy. In faith, I do not believe that she loves him either. But Mr. Collins's self-assurance will not perceive any other reality than the reality that he places over his own eyes.

My parents feel as if I avoided an awkward fate that would never have made me happy. I now see the same.

I say this now because I am safe too. Lizzy, there was a time where I had considered accepting Mr. Collins's hand in marriage. For a fleeting moment, when he proposed, I entertained the idea of accepting him.

Imagine if I had said yes! What a fate I would have shackled myself to. Thank goodness I kept my wits about me.

Now, despite all the manifold advantages that I would have inherited from our match, I have no regrets.

Maria is now being courted by Mr. Long's nephew, who had come into town. He actually is landed gentry in Surrey and has a nice country seat. My brother, Gregory, is also amidst a courtship with Mr. King's sister-in-law, who has a respectable dowry, and he is making plans to be a midshipman in the Navy. My eldest brother will inherit Lucas Lodge, and he has no plans of marrying, so he will need me to help run the household. I shall fall somewhere, better than I would have fallen if I had married your cousin.

Elizabeth, I don't think that I ever wish to get married. It is just...not who I am. If it ever was.

I miss you, dear friend.
Other than what I have mentioned, Hertfordshire
remains one of the best places on earth.
Hope you are well and please write to me soon.

C.L.

When I closed the letter, I felt elated.

"Lizzy, the rice!" Kitty cried.

The rice began to boil over.

"Right!" I cried. I tended to it immediately and stirred it till the water stopped boiling. "Never fear, I got it. All is well."

"What did Charlotte write about that turned your head?"

"She is not angry with me. She knows what she did was right." I laughed. "She is *not angry* with me."

"Of course, she isn't," Jane voiced. "She never could be."

"I know. It's just nice to hear it."

We sat down to dinner and began to eat. As we did so, Jane began to tell us of the children who she looked after.

"The Kirkpatrick sons are as lively as ever," Jane said. "Getting them to sit still is not the easiest thing, nor is it getting any easier. But they both are lovely boys, who have large hearts. The eldest is Master Oswald[1], and the second is Master Rodger. Little Rodger is not as handsome as Master Oswald, but I like Master Rodger a little more. He is very interested in nature and is always asking me about the creatures that I saw in the country. I wish that I could take him back to Longbourn and have him run amongst the hills, plains, rivers, and streams, so that he could see everything. The poor thing would be so much happier

---

1. Oswald, Rodger, and Cynthia are all names taken from characters in *Wives & Daughters*.

in the grass and dirt. And then there is the difficult situation; the daughter."

"What?" I asked. "Is she unruly?"

"She has a distinct personality, which is very sweet, but her mother doesn't seem to have much interest in her. Her mother loves her—to the best of her ability. But little Cynthia deserves more."

"The girl's name is Cynthia?"

"Yes. Her name comes from her mother, Hyacinth."

"Hyacinth?" I asked, with a raised eyebrow. "Now that is a unique name."

"I like it, but the stuffier parts of the country would find a natural prejudice toward her."

"I noticed that," Kitty remarked, "people have problems with the stupidest things to have problems with."

"True," I supported.

"Well, little Cynthia is a lovely girl with obvious winning ways, but she needs a friend. Her life is so secluded and confined to the classroom, that she has no acquaintances with other children, especially with other little girls."

This sparked my interest.

"This Mr. and Mrs. Kirkpatrick," I inquired, "do they have any prejudices of who their children associate with? Nationality or class preferences? For I know a little girl, who is very lovely, but her parents are gone, and she is raised by her uncle, who is a professor. And she is from Australia. Her name is Molly Gibson."

"Well, I cannot say for certain if my employers have such preferences, but I can always speak to them about it. Mrs. Kirkpatrick can be reasonable, and if you come with this Miss Gibson and visit her home one day, then it might work."

I smirked.

"A plan is afoot. I wish, for one moment, my brain would stop working. But this is who I am!"

I chuckled and kept eating.

Later that evening, Jane and I were in bed, amidst falling asleep.

"Lizzy?" Jane asked me as she was facing the wall, looking away from me.

"Yes?"

"Whenever you speak to Mr. Darcy, does he ever mention Mr. Bingley?"

"No," I lied. "He does not."

"Oh."

"Should I ask him about it?"

"No. I do not want you to embarrass yourself."

"I'll ask him."

"Thank you."

"You did want me to say something, didn't you?"

"Yes."

Sometimes, in life, it's all about reading the words through people's silence on things.

Chapter 21

Staying Indefinitely

While the Bennet sisters ate at home, Darcy spent his evening in another fashion.

When Mr. Darcy dressed for his dinner with Mr. Thornton, Mr. Jefferson entered to tell him that he got a letter from Mr. Bingley.

To be on time, Darcy ordered the letter to be placed in his coat. When he finished dressing, he had his carriage brought round to the front of the hotel.

On his way to Marlborough Mills, Darcy opened the letter and began to read it. The contents of the letter made him smile.

Dear Darcy,

All is forgiven. You were looking ~~at~~ after my welfare, and I appreciate that. I do not deny that I wish that you ~~had~~ hadn't interfered, for it may have marred my chances with her. But since you have informed me that she has no romantic prospects, perhaps she can forgive me as well.

I will never begrudge you, Darcy, for being a gra—great friend. You know me; when I ~~choi~~ choose to do something, it is done in the work of ~~of~~ a moment. If this letter precedes me, then know that I shall be at Milton by next Monday.

*Look forward to my coming, for I shall check in at the
hotel by then and I will need you to call on me for when I
need to find Miss Bennet. I shall need your help. I know that
I shall have it.*

C. Bingley

Darcy closed the letter, not surprised at seeing some words
scratched out in it. All was beginning to be put to rights. Now
he only needed to clear his name with Miss Elizabeth. He
would begin again tomorrow.

When he arrived at Thornton's house for dinner, Mrs.
Thornton was happy to see him, but it was Fanny Thornton
who was very much the happiest.

"How lovely your cravat is arranged," she complimented
him.

"Thank you, Miss Thornton," Darcy responded.

"How rarely we see men dressed in such an aesthetic way."

"Thank you. You are looking lovely this evening."

"Thank you." She chuckled. "I send away for all the latest
fashions from London. I firmly believe that I cannot go to
London, so I had darn well better dress like I was on my way
there."

"Still a desire to see London?"

"Always. I still have not been to London, and it hurts.
Believe me, Mr. Darcy, if you lived in such a dirty and smoky
place, you wouldn't be able to wait to leave. Especially if you
were delicate, such as myself. Yes, I am very delicate. And I am
sure that all this smoke is not beneficial to my health."

"Let's all sit down to dinner now," Mr. Thornton responded,
to put an end to Fanny's talks about her health.

As they sat down, Mr. Darcy was able to inspect Mrs.

Thornton, and saw that nothing was anything else but customary. She wore the same handsome dress in stout black silk, of which not a thread was worn or discolored. When Fanny had been talking, she was mending a long tablecloth of the finest texture, holding it up against the light occasionally to discover thin places, which required her delicate care.

Everything in the room, as always, was perfectly in place. But it was all still, and there was nothing feminine about it. Such a contrast to the Bennet residence, which was small, entirely feminine, but not being against the male touch.

As they ate, Mrs. Thornton asked Darcy how much longer they would have the pleasure of his company. There was no emotion when she said this, but Darcy knew that no offense was given. Mrs. Thornton was happy that he was there. It merely wasn't her habit to display emotion, even when she felt it.

"At the moment," Darcy answered, "I plan to stay indefinitely, until I have fulfilled my purpose in coming."

"And what is your purpose?" Miss Thornton asked.

"Fanny," Mrs. Thornton chided, "it is not our right to inquire."

"Thank you, Mrs. Thornton. Miss Thornton, my purpose in coming is innocent and is merely the desire to reconnect with an acquaintance of mine who I wish to assist in her recovery."

"What lady?" Fanny asked. Her spirit was alight. She had hoped, deep down, that Mr. Darcy might have been referring to herself. Imagine her disappointment when the truth will out!

"A Miss Elizabeth Bennet, from Longbourn."

"Oh," Fanny replied, looking a little disappointed. Although her expression soon shifted to one of familiarity. "Jane's sister?"

"Yes."

"Bennet!" Thornton gasped.

"John?" Mrs. Thornton questioned.

"Nothing, Mother. I just recalled something. I saw Miss Elizabeth Bennet today."

"Did you?" Darcy asked.

"Yes. When I visited Mr. Hale. She was Miss Hale's company."

"You've spoken a lot about Mr. Hale since you met him, John," Mrs. Thornton responded. Then she turned to Mr. Darcy. "To the point where he wishes for us to pay a visit."

"It is merely out of friendship," Thornton responded, "I admire Mr. Hale. He is a gentleman and I feel an ease around him. And his wife and daughter are ladies."

Mrs. Thornton's eye turned weary. Ah! A mother who was worried about her son being taken in.

"Do they teach too?" she asked. "What do they do? You have never mentioned them."

"No, they do not teach. I have never seen Mrs. Hale, but I have only met Miss Hale twice and each time was less than half an hour."

"Take care you don't get caught by a penniless girl, John."

Her mother bit into her food and Darcy could not help being interested in this discussion. After all, he had given Bingley the same advice that Mrs. Thornton was giving her son. And now he was encouraging the match. How the tides had turned!

"I am not easily caught, Mother," Thornton responded, "as I think you know. But I must not have Miss Hale spoken of in that way, which, you know, is offensive to me. I never was aware of any young lady trying to catch me yet, nor do I believe that anyone has ever given themselves that useless trouble."

"Well! I only say, take care. Perhaps our Milton girls have too much spirit and good feeling to go angling after husbands. But this Miss Hale comes out of the aristocratic counties, where, if all tales be true, rich husbands are reckoned prizes."

Darcy scratched his chin, thinking of Elizabeth. He had found the one woman in England who did not view him as a prize.

Thornton clearly looked disconcerted by his mother's comment.

"Mother," he replied, laughing a little, "you will make me confess. The only times that I saw Miss Hale, she treated me with a strong flavor of contempt in it. She held herself over me as if she had been a queen, and I'm an offending vassal. I am safe from her, and you may rest easy."

"No, I may not rest easy, nor be content either. What business had she, a renegade clergyman's daughter, to turn up her nose at you? I would dress for none of them—a saucy set! And I only visit for your own wishes, John, and nothing more."

Fanny laughed at this.

"Mr. Hale is good, and gentle and learned," Thornton objected. "He is not saucy."

"But Miss Hale despises you? Humph! I should like to know why. I am your mother, yes, but I can see what's what, and not be blinded by favoritism. You are nobler than any other man this Miss Hale would ever find. Despise you? I hate her for it."

Mr. Darcy's eyes widened, and he continued to eat his food. Rather, he was secretly amused, and so was Thornton.

"First, Miss Hale is guilty *for* taking a fancy to me," Thornton observed, "and now she is guilty *for not* taking a fancy to me." He laughed. "Mama, what can she do that will have you forgive her?"

"Like you," Mrs. Thornton responded, "but understand that she has no right to do anything about it. It is simple."

Thornton and Darcy exchanged a look: both saw the humor in this.

After dinner, the gentlemen separated and went to the other room, to speak. While there, Darcy took advantage of this opportunity.

"Thornton, I must ask a favor of you."

"What?"

"I do not know for how long I shall remain in Milton, but I know that it would be longer than I would like. And it is longer than I would prefer to remain at a hotel. I was wondering, if you wouldn't mind, can I pay you rent and remain here at Marlborough Mills?"

"Oh, Darcy, that is the request?"

"Yes."

"I cannot ask you to pay rent. You must be my guest."

"That is why I didn't ask you, but I offered it. You are a manufacturer. The last thing you need is a rich man living off you. Once I have your acceptance, I am going to offer my payments to Mrs. Thornton. Your mother is a practical woman; she will accept my fees."

"Yes, mama would do that. My practical mother!"

"Yes."

"Darcy, I must ask. Your staying so long...would it have to do with the Bennet sisters?"

"Yes. One in particular."

"Miss Elizabeth?"

"Yes."

Mr. Thornton sat down, rubbing his eyes. This did not escape Darcy's notice.

"Thornton, what is that look for?"

"Like I said, I met her."

"Yes." Darcy was adept at reading into Thornton's expressions and looking past his stern gaze. After all, Darcy's face moved in the same fashion. "Thornton, what did you do?"

"I met her twice, while she was with her friend, Miss Hale."

"Yes."

"And I firmly believe that both women might despise me."

"Despise you?"

"Yes."

"Whatever for?"

"I believe that... I made a bad second impression. After the first bad impression."

It was now Mr. Darcy's turn to rub his eyes. It was as if Thornton had found Darcy's own secret shame and began to share it.

"Oh," Darcy responded, and he sat down next to Thornton. "Very well. Tell me what happened."

Thornton told Darcy everything.

Chapter 22

The Truth

Able to take time in between my classes, I had been able to go to Milton Court, which was where the regiment would enter Milton. When I had done so, there were many people crowding around both sides of the street. When I did go there, I managed to run into Kitty and Raspberry. They were wearing their chambermaid uniforms under their coats and bonnets.

"Lizzy!" Kitty cried when seeing me, "we're here!"

I ran up to them and they pulled my hand.

"We have a perfect spot," Raspberry said, and then we moved through the crowd. As we did so, I accidentally knocked into a young and thin woman with straight blonde hair. I knocked her shawl off her shoulder.

"I am sorry," I said going to pick it up.

"It's all well," she said, "thank yer."

When I looked at her, I saw that I recognized her.

"I know your face," I observed. "Don't you work at Marlborough Mills?"

"Yea, yer saw me when you faced down Thornton. My name is Bessie."

"I'm Elizabeth."

"Lizzy," Kitty said, pulling me away from Bessie so that we could get a better view. Tearing my eyes away from Bessie, I joined Kitty and Raspberry as we found a spot to the front of the crowd.

In less than a couple of minutes, the regiment began to march through the town. Seeing them made us all giddy and we all cheered.

"They are handsome, aren't they?" Raspberry said. "Wait, there's Plato!"

We followed where she pointed, and there he was, of medium brown skin amongst his lighter company. Seeing Plato solved every reason for how he became a soldier. He was tall, handsome and he looked like a leader. If he had been born to any other reality of time, he might have been a king.

"He looks handsome," Kitty realized, equally as astonished as I was.

"You sound surprised."

"Sorry, but yes, I am."

"Kitty!" I gasped. "Look! There's Denny, Captain Carter, and Sanderson!"

She scanned the regiment and she saw them. It was the most exhilarating thing.

"I see them!" she cried. "I see them! That means that Lydia is here too."

We all stood there, marveling at the officers marching through the streets.

"Remember when it was like this?" Kitty whispered to me. "Remember those days?"

"Yes," I professed. "But it's more than that. Kitty, for one moment, it feels as if Hertfordshire has come to Milton."

"I know. This is the best that we can hope for now."

I couldn't stay more than a couple of minutes, because I had to return to work.

I managed to make it back to Granger Hall just in time. Which was good because it was Mr. Dennison that I was taking notes for. Both he and I had a silent agreement to not speak to each other. So, I sat there and took notes the entire time. When I finished, he stormed out of the hall so that we would have no chance to speak.

That was fine by me.

Going back to the offices, I sat down and rewrote my notes, then I received word that a gentleman was waiting for me. Curious about this, I put my coat and bonnet on and left the office. My surprise was slight, but still genuine, when I saw Mr. Darcy standing there.

"Mr. Darcy!"

"Good day, Miss Bennet."

"It's a pleasure to see you."

"Thank you. I was wondering if you would prefer another ride home."

"Only if it is of no inconvenience to you."

"I can assure you, it is not."

"Then I will accept."

We left the hall and soon were on our way to Frances Street.

"Miss Bennet," he began, "I must apologize for how my behavior was when last we met. And my reaction to seeing your new residence."

"Thank you, but there is nothing to apologize for," I assured him. "I am aware of your feelings. You've made them plain. Your reaction was merely that of a man who was surprised and cared. You cared for our welfare. Whatever our disagreements, I am sensitive to that. I took no offense."

"Thank you. But to what you said before of our past disagreements—I wish to talk of that. There is something there that we must face."

"Mr. Darcy, are you about to ask me about your proposal? If

so, I am prepared, and you can tell me anything. And, regarding the matter, I have news about my sister toward Mr. Bingley."

"No. I wish to have you tell me what Mr. Wickham told you that I did to him."

"Ah."

"I am prepared."

I steadied out my breathing and began.

"He told me about his misfortunes. Of how you robbed him of his inheritance. Of how your father, who favored him, granted him a living in his will, of offering Mr. Wickham the living at Kempton Parsonage, as a clergyman. And how, when your father died, you refused, pointblank, to honor your father's wishes. And you offered the living to someone else, reducing him to his state of poverty."

"He said that!" Mr. Darcy hissed.

"Yes. Do you deny it?"

"With every part of my soul. Miss Bennet, I know that Mr. Wickham is very capable of making anyone believe in his lies, but lies they are, and I have evidence to prove it. First, yes, he was given the living in my father's will. But it was left to him, in condition, only. But he did not live the life of a man who is meant for the church. Wickham is a gambler, and he loves women, but does not honor them. He has had...dalliances with ladies who deserved a better fate than he offered them. His appetites were not what they ought to have been.

"Secondly, when my father died, it was Wickham who refused the living at Kempton. Instead, he requested and was granted 3,000 pounds instead of the living. I was happy that he chose this route, for I was happy to be rid of him. How he lived, I know not, but I do know that he gambled away the money in weeks. Eventually, he returned to Pemberley and demanded more money of me. When I refused, he grew angry, and little did I know that he sought revenge. My sister, Georgiana, was but fifteen years old at the time. She was staying in Ramsgate with a companion named Mrs. Younge, in whose character we were all unhappily deceived. Soon, Mr. Wickham followed Georgiana there, under Mrs. Younge's information, and he endeared himself to Georgiana so much, that he convinced her to consent to an elopement—his object being her 50,000 pounds. Fortunately, I arrived there the day before their elopement, and Georgiana told me everything. I was angry and disgusted. And when I told Mr. Wickham that, if he married Georgiana, he would never receive any of the money, he quitted the place immediately and abandoned her. That was the last I had seen of Mr. Wickham. Until I saw him walking with you all, in Meryton."

I felt my heart bursting in my chest.

"This cannot be true?" I gasped.

"It is. Miss Bennet. Would I lie about something like that happening to my sister? You know I prefer the truth behind all things."

"Yes, I know you do, but...but..."

I leaned back and thought about it.

"And to the truth of it, you can appeal to Colonel Fitzwilliam, who will confirm everything that I had said."

"Yes," I whispered, "you are no liar. But can this be true? A part of me doesn't want to believe it."

"Wickham is very good at making others love him. While I am not."

I felt cold as many thoughts and sensations dashed across my mind. There was the very real possibility that I was grossly in error. And feeling its veracity hurt!

"I...this means that I was wrong. This means that I allowed myself to be deceived. I blamed you for things that you weren't guilty of. You wouldn't lie about something like that."

"No, I wouldn't."

I was horrified.

"Yes," I whispered. "This is all true. Isn't it?"

"Yes, it is."

"Then this means... I trusted evil. I trusted a liar. I deceived myself." The shame rose up in me so fast, that I clung to committing a rash and abrupt course of action. "Please stop the carriage."

"Why?"

"I don't want you to see me like this. I want to walk. I am mortified."

"Miss Bennet, please do not propose such. What man would I be for making you walk the rest of the way home?"

"I don't deserve this!" I cried. "I don't want you looking at me while I am so ashamed."

"But I will not let you despise yourself to such a degree. I didn't tell you this to make you hate yourself. I told you this so that you would know me better and to shield you from a lie."

"Yes," I quieted down. "Forgive me, I was being nonsensical. My apologies, but I do not wish to speak for the rest of the ride home. I know that you did this to enlighten me, and you have saved me from my own misunderstanding. I can see that now, but for the rest of me, you don't know what it's like. You don't know what it's like to sit in a carriage knowing that you wronged the other person. That you hurt them. That you were entirely wrong about everything. Please, I don't want you to see me in this way."

"Very well."

We rode the rest of the way in silence. Eventually, we pulled up to my house, Darcy stepped down and offered me his hand. Taking it, I allowed him to help me down.

"Mr. Darcy," I breathed in, unable to face him. "Thank you for the ride."

"It was my pleasure."

"And thank you for telling me the truth. I just... I need time to face myself."

"How much time?"

"I shall tell you soon."

"Very well. I shall have to be contented with that."

"But understand this... I am very sorry for what I believed."

He nodded to me.

He got back into his carriage and rode off.

After he left, I ran into my house—my small house—ran upstairs to my bed and fell into it, in despair.

It must all be true.

Would Darcy lie about so much?

About his sister?

His father's will!

Of course not! And the more that I contemplated the matter, the more that all veracity leaned toward him. Mr. Wickham's tale was filled with lies, and it showed how blind I was. There was no way that Darcy could have robbed him of his inheritance because Wickham could have easily challenged it with legal address. Every time that Darcy entered society, Wickham shirked away like a retreating cretin. He only spoke ill of Darcy when Darcy was not there. If he was in the right, then he would have stood his ground. But he ran every time. He was a coward. Had I actually been in love with him, I could not have been more blind. But at least love would have been an excuse. But it wasn't! I was never in love with Mr. Wickham. So, my only excuse was the bad first impression that Darcy had left me.

And now, all of that had been done away in view of everything.

I chose the man who did not love me, over the man who did.

And I didn't even love the man who didn't love me at all. How backwards it all was!

And to add to all of this, Mr. Darcy had proven himself to be a very sincere man, intelligent, genuine, passionate, and who did improve on closer acquaintance.

If I had given him a chance, and opened my heart to him, not only could I be married to a man who I respected, and who loved me, but who also could keep my sisters safe from destitution.

And now, here I was, in Milton, with my sisters trying to make a living for themselves in a station that they were not born into.

We are factory women.

Chambermaids.

Notetakers.

Governesses.

All are noble professions, but we have very little savings, we must always struggle, and we are always thrown into the dangers of the unknown.

I could have fallen in love with a good man.

But I deceived myself. And by so doing, I ruined my sisters at the same time.

I had wronged myself.

I had offended myself.

Ruined myself.

I was... the villain of this moment.

End of Book I

Hello Readers,

I hope that you enjoyed Book I of the Austen Gaskell Series. You all are gems for reading this, and I know that there may be a few questions about why I did this crossover.

Why have the *Pride and Prejudice* characters mix with the *North and South* ones?

For those who have either read or seen both versions, you might be like me and have noted the similarities to both stories. While one being Regency and in lighter tones, and one being Victorian, but with darker tones, the romance between the heroes and heroines has that same passionate fire to it of misunderstandings, preconceptions, pride, and prejudice. Long have I thought about the similarities, so I wondered, what would happen if the characters met?

Why more focus on Miss Austen's characters over Miss Gaskell's?

Readers, I can assure you that this was a deliberate choice, but NOT to undermine Miss Gaskell's work. It is merely that, first, since Miss Austen's work was the first one written and published (due to generation), it made sense to begin with her work. Also, *Pride and Prejudice* is more commonly read. If a reader wished to pick up this novel, curious, but is not so familiar with Miss Gaskell's work, then I wanted to take my time and help them get more acquainted with the story of Milton, through Miss Austen's characters. If you have never read *North and South*, never fear, there is no judgment at all. Life is busy; we all don't get the time to read as much as we wish. I still haven't gotten around to reading *The Help* or *The Davinci Code*. Such is life. That being said, I would recommend at least watching the BBC adaptation of *North and South*, written by Sandy Welch. She adapted it very well, and I think you would enjoy it.

For those of you who are aware of my tendency to see actors

in my brain when I write my work, then yes, I totally saw all the actors from that series when I was writing.

But for those who are apprehensive about me not including much of North and South, I promise that the entire novel will be covered throughout this series.

Why did I have Mr. Thornton and Margaret Hale meet in the way that I did?

For those who have read the novel and watched the series, you would know that Sandy Welch had the hero and heroine meet in an entirely different way than in the book. I chose to do a slight variation on how Miss Welch did it in the miniseries, rather than adhere to the book, because I thought that it was a stronger introduction to the characters, as well as Miss Welch did a good job at establishing the prejudice that Margaret would have had against Mr. Thornton. It gave Margaret's feelings stronger validation. Mind you, I still love the way the characters met in the novel, of course. I just thought Miss Welch did a great job of establishing it in a way that was very relatable.

Why do I write my books in series, rather than just one long book?

This actually has to do with experience. When I was growing up, I loved reading books that were a series. It always gave me something to look forward to. Also, I grew up in the time where all books were hardcopy or paperback. The bigger the book, the more room it took up in your bag. One time, I asked my dad for the first three books in the Chronicles of Narnia series, so that they would be easier to carry. Instead of listening to that, he bought me the collected works of the entire series (in one book form). That book was hell to carry. It got to the point where I never finished the book series because it was just too cumbersome to walk around with. Despite that Kindle makes it easier, my mind is just so cemented in the pleasures of a series, as well as the convenience of it not being very large, that I will always be in that mentality.

Also, if you buy a book, but don't like it, at least it's not too long. So, when a book is of a moderate length, at least you can finish it, before you throw it aside and say, 'oh dear!'

What is with the lack of romance?

I assure you all, as the series progresses, the romance will increase. The first book is to establish the story, but the characters will develop over time. I wish, with my all heart, that I had the writing skill to give immediate romance while also developing a plot, but for the life of me, I DON'T have that talent. I really wish I could though. Sometimes, we just have to make do with the little bit of skill that we've got.

Who is Molly Gibson, and the Kirkpatrick Children?

There are children in this tale: Mr. Hanley's niece, Molly Gibson, and the Kirkpatrick children: Oswald, Roger, and Cynthia.

These are all child versions of characters from Miss Gaskell's other work 'Wives and Daughters.' So, this is a combination of 'Pride & Prejudice', 'North and South,' with a touch of 'Wives and Daughters.'

Why the cultural diversity? Is there an agenda to this?

The reasons for this are manifold. First, Raspberry is a nod back to Miss Austen's part-mulatto character in Sanditon, Miss Lambe. That book, like much of her writing, was showing us how Jane was willing to adapt with her times and how she was always about going forward in life. Since Miss Austen was adapting to change and showing that she was open to new ideas, it was fitting to progress alongside her.

Second, it's just to be realistic.

The Bennets are now living in cosmopolitan England, as opposed to rural England. When this occurs, they are going to have a wider view with the ways of the world. In cities, there was more diversity, more encounter with foreigners, etc. It's about simply letting everyone in.

This choice ties in with an event that occurs later in *North and South*. Miss Gaskell's book makes heavy references into the idea of 'foreigners,' rejecting people of differences, and even the heroine sometimes adheres to prejudices in her day. There is one particular event in her novel, where there is a crisis over this. I plan to have the Bennet sisters involved in this. By having the Bennets face diverse characters in their lives, it is there to justify their sympathy for characters later, in Miss Gaskell's novel. Also, in *North and South*, the 'idea' and 'concept' of foreigners was a theme that was often brought up. It's best to sometimes have some consistency to an original work.

Will there be a sequel?

I have every intention of there being one. When I first wrote this four years ago, I wrote it to be audience dependent. If audiences don't like it, I don't continue. Since they did, I continued.

As you all know, my readers are everything to me.

Reader, thank you so much. See you soon!

Don't miss out on your next favorite book!

Join the Satin Romance mailing list
www.satinromance.com/mail.html

THANK YOU FOR READING

Did you enjoy this book?

We invite you to leave a review at your favorite book site, such as Goodreads, Amazon, Barnes & Noble, etc.

DID YOU KNOW THAT LEAVING A REVIEW...

- Helps other readers find books they may enjoy.
- Gives you a chance to let your voice be heard.
- Gives authors recognition for their hard work.
- Doesn't have to be long. A sentence or two about why you liked the book will do.

About the Author

Ney Mitch has been a long-standing Jane Austen enthusiast, having written forty novels that were inspired by her various works. Since stumbling on Miss Austen's books after graduating from college, she has always dabbled in Austen inspired literature, ranging from writing works for teens to adults. Originally, her desire was to adapt Jane Austen's writing in a way to help young adults connect with her, however over time, she has spread her aims to other genres and styles. Having received her BA Degree at Desales University, she is a writer, both literary and dramatic, as well as being a Historic Reenactor.

f facebook.com/courtney.mitchell.589

X x.com/CMMitchelPsyche

P pinterest.com/shebaanna

Also by Ney Mitch
with Satin Romance

Austen Gaskell Series
Curiosities & Contemplation

Kitty Bennet Adventure Series
Vanities & Vexations

Forms & Fashions

Romance & Recklessness

Nuance & Novelty

Romance & Revolution Saga
The First Impression

The Memory Series
Moments of Moments Past

Moments of Moments Present

Moments of Moments Future

Moments of Moments Infinite

Pride & Prejudice Reimaginings
Rapture & Rebellion

Fortune & Misfortune

Desire & Destiny

Pride & Peace

Resolve & Revelations

Hope & Hopelessness

Chances Series

Chances Are

Chances Come

Chances Fade

Chances End

Novels

The Tale of Mr. & Mrs. Bennet: A Pride & Prejudice Christmas Tale

Considerations Near Christmastime